When Adam Opens His Eyes

Titles in the Library of Korean Literature
available from Dalkey Archive Press

1. *Stingray*
Kim Joo-young

2. *One Spoon on This Earth*
Hyun Ki Young

3. *When Adam Opens His Eyes*
Jang Jung-il

4. *My Son's Girlfriend*
Jung Mi-kyung

5. *A Most Ambiguous Sunday, and Other Stories*
Jung Young Moon

6. *The House with a Sunken Courtyard*
Kim Won-il

7. *At Least We Can Apologize*
Lee Ki-ho

8. *The Soil*
Yi Kwang-su

9. *Lonesome You*
Park Wan-suh

10. *No One Writes Back*
Jang Eun-jin

LIBRARY OF KOREAN LITERATURE
3

When Adam Opens His Eyes

Jang Jung-il

Translated by
Hwang Sun-Ae *and*
Horace Jeffery Hodges

DALKEY ARCHIVE PRESS
CHAMPAIGN / LONDON / DUBLIN

Originally published in Korean as *Adam i nun ttŭl ttae* by Kimyŏngsa, Seoul, 1990

Library of Congress Cataloging-in-Publication Data

Chang, Chong-il, 1962-
[Adam i nun ttul ttae. English]
When Adam Opens His Eyes / Jang Jung-il ; translated by Hwang Sun-ae and Horace Jeffery Hodges.
pages cm
ISBN 978-1-56478-914-3 (alk. paper)
1. Korea--Fiction. 2. Bildungsromans. gsafd I. Hwang, Son-ae, translator. II. Hodges, Horace Jeffery, translator. III. Title.
PL992.14.C47A313 2013
895.7'34--dc23
2013027223

Partially funded by a grant from the Illinois Arts Council, a state agency

Library of Korean Literature
Published in collaboration with the Literature Translation Institute of Korea

www.dalkeyarchive.com

Cover: design and composition by Mikhail Iliatov

Thanks to Wei-Ling Woo of Epigram Books (Singapore)
for helping with the editing of this book.

Printed on permanent/durable acid-free paper

I was nineteen years old, and the things that I most wanted to have were a typewriter, prints of Munch's paintings and a turntable for playing records. Those things alone were all that I wanted from this world when I was nineteen. But so humble were my desires that, in comparison, my mother's wish for me to enter Seoul National University, or my younger cousin's dream of joining the Samsung Lions baseball team when he grew up, seemed even more out of reach.

If my desires hadn't been for such trivial things, but for something larger like becoming the president, I could easily have fulfilled that desire by driving a tank or randomly firing an M16. Or I could have fulfilled it deep in the night by ejaculating in a wet dream. Or by giving up completely. I mean, I could have fulfilled my dream simply by throwing it away. In the sense of being freed from the desire, completely giving up might be nothing but my desire's fulfillment. So whoever discovers how to empty himself of all desire will become a free person, one who controls himself so perfectly that he becomes his own master.

That year, I failed to gain admittance to the university my mother wished for me in the major that I wanted to study, and I began cramming for the next year's entrance exam. Sending a child to university was hard for a poor family, and supporting him for an extra year of cramming was even harder. Not only was the cost of repeated tutoring hard to bear, but even worse was the gossip of close relatives who sometimes dropped in or neighbors who lived in the same one-story building paying monthly rent for cramped quarters. At that time, my mother was working downtown as a cleaning lady in an underground shopping area.

After I failed by only seven or eight points to gain admission to the English department at the university, I briefly considered going to any of the provincial universities in my hometown that would offer a scholarship, but I decided to accept my older brother's advice. The reason that I found his advice persuasive was that an extra year cramming for the entrance exam had gotten him admitted to business school in the university that I had applied to. Besides, I was hardheaded enough to insist on meeting my own stubborn goal. Even if that aim was first expected of me by my mother, why shouldn't we do a favor for our parents, who gave us life?

Cramming an extra year for another test means becoming a lonely student. There's an old saying that women in olden times had to live for three years mute, three years blind, and three years deaf while living with their in-laws. An extra year of cramming is not much different. I realized this acutely upon seeing that my exam number was missing from the list of successful candidates. From that moment of failure, I was estranged from the world.

For a month after the announcement, I could not face my friend Eun-sun. I even feared getting a call from her. My fear, I admit, was a kind of shame, but a teenager's fear of the other sex often stems from shamefulness, so the fear is easily understood. Although we had been friends from the eleventh grade and were close enough to overlook each other's faults, I still could not free myself from the shame of failure. In fact, for the first month, I tried especially hard to avoid everyone close to me. I could hardly even sit at the dinner table with my mother.

The very day after successful candidates had been announced, I registered at a "cram school" in an area downtown that was thick with these institutes devoted to helping students cram another year for the university entrance exam. I had become so used to this style of learning in my past three years of high school, so deadened to everything else in life, especially during my senior year, that I would have felt crippled if forced to live differently. Just looking away from my books and notebooks for a brief moment was enough to give me feelings of insecurity and anxious helplessness. As I later discovered, those who failed the exam and immediately registered at a cram school were usually people suffering from delusions of persecution, just like me.

At the cram school I attended, many other students who had become crammers the day before were registering for courses. Only then was I able to escape from my shame that I alone had failed the university entrance exam. I felt freed from that desolate sense of failure, of groundlessness, of having stumbled at life's starting gate and been left behind by others at the first step.

Only into the second month of cram school did I get Eun-sun's phone call and take up her suggestion to meet. I had grown so sick of cramming after barely a month and a half that I found myself cursing unconsciously. High school might have resembled a cottage industry to ready us for university, but the cram school was a large, mechanized factory with conveyor belts running continuously. No humanity existed there. For the first time, I grew skeptical about learning. What kind of learning was this in which memorizing facts and repeating exercises would get one a perfect score?

I met Eun-sun at a tearoom. Since we'd last met, she'd learned how to drink coffee in quite an elegant manner. Like an actress in a television ad, she lifted her cup delicately, drank with poise, and smiled softly.

"Could you have a look at this?" she asked. "I'd like to be a published and recognized poet no later than the end of this summer."

Eun-sun and I had first met in the eleventh grade at an

exhibition for poetry and painting hosted by her school's literary club. Now, as well as then, a high school exhibition of poetry and painting was one of the few officially acknowledged places where students could meet members of the other sex. It was there that I discovered a lovely poem that immediately caught my eye. It had been written by Eun-sun.

"Did you write the poem 'An Inferior Student'?" I had asked.

"Yes, I did."

I was meeting Eun-sun for the first time, a girl with a face and name unknown to me until the club president, who had invited me to the exhibition, pointed her out when I asked who had written that poem.

"It's not bad, your poem."

"People think that I copied it."

When I had approached her that first time to talk, she had responded indifferently. She seemed to have little interest in the exhibition, even appearing a bit irritated.

"You mean the 'The Inferior Student,' by Prévert?" I asked.

"Yes."

I could understand her irritation. Her poem was similar to Prévert's only in the title. No, actually in their nuance, the one Eun-sun had written and "The Inferior Student" by Prévert were also somewhat similar. But Eun-sun's poem was more honest and intense. Maybe more modern. I had that impression not only in comparison with Prévert's poem, but also compared to the scribblings by all the other high school poets. Together with her, I returned to her poem and read it again:

> Writing a poem in math class,
> I get thumped on the head by the teacher.
>
> Writing a poem in science class,
> I get caned on my palms by the teacher.

Writing a poem in social studies class,
I get ridiculed by the teacher.

Writing a poem in Korean class,
I get reprimanded by the teacher.

I don't like teachers.
All the teachers in the world, I
Hate them, so writes
An inferior student.

Turning from the poem to Eun-sun, I told her, "Not bad. It's more honest, more intense, and more modern."

Eun-sun was a person with a strong sense of pride and even seemed upset at my careful comments. I felt quite sure that they upset her.

"Compared with Prévert? My God. I've never read anything by someone like Prévert!"

"I know. If you had read his poem, you wouldn't have been able to write a better one. Should we introduce ourselves? I am—"

"I already know your name."

I felt flattered. I was well-known in the city's high school literary scene. But embarrassment followed immediately, and I blushed to discover that a stranger knew who I was.

"Aren't you participating in literary competitions these days?" she asked, her voice taking on a very polite tone.

I was a literary guy, specializing in literary competitions. About once every two months, I would take part in these competitions for high school students organized by various universities or by various cities and provinces. I had even entered a high school magazine's contest for a literary prize. At the peak of my career, I was perhaps winning prizes in about half the competitions I entered. Because she had suddenly adopted a very polite tone, our conversation became somewhat awkward.

"I'm trying to learn something these days," I finally replied.

"You mean for school?" Her eyes grew big and round with surprise.

Relaxing for the first time, I observed her face closely. She had a prominent forehead, appealing creases on her upper eyelids, and dark eyebrows. Her lips were full and her nose bridge high, as if she were part Spanish or Latin American. Not quite a beauty but almost, because her face was unusual, and there was nothing displeasing about it. She was the most attractive girl that I had met in my seventeen years.

"For literary criticism," I told her.

"As a high school student?"

I had told my friends in the literary club that I was busy studying literary criticism, but I had lied, for I wasn't really doing that. My friends were expecting me to write great literary criticism, but I was just using the story as an excuse. I had grown tired of being dragged off to represent my school at literary competitions. I needed rest. Besides, I didn't want to fail the university exam as a result of spending all my study time on creative writing. Whenever I skipped school for literary competitions and had to spend time writing poems, my mother's worried face appeared before my eyes in vivid detail.

"What do you think?" Eun-sun asked, bringing me back to the present. "Are they good enough? Where should I send them? Evidently, a poetry magazine would be best, wouldn't it?"

Showing me about twenty poems that she had written in the twelve months since the previous winter, she asked me these four baited questions.

She then added, "I would like to be recognized as a poet as quickly as possible so that I can enjoy my time in university. How wonderful that would be! A freshman, yet debuting on the literary stage!"

Perfection usually does not go well with selfishness and vanity.

Whatever the perfection, vanity is like an ill-fitting garment. But for this youngest daughter whose father held a high position in the local civil service, vanity and selfishness fit as perfectly as skin on the body.

"Well, these sound too professional, I think."

On the day that we had first met, I bought her a pocketbook of Prévert's poetry. The name "Prévert" still brings to mind fresh memories of our encounter that day. Had she already grown sick of that? As if finding the memory abhorrent, she said in a critical tone, "Again like Prévert?"

"No," I told her. "Except for a few, all are in the style of Choi Seung-ja."

Perhaps I had understood the secret of her poetry from the beginning. Eun-sun had been holding a book of Choi Seung-ja's poems at that poetry and painting exhibition when we were in the eleventh grade and had never put it away since then. To read Choi Seung-ja as a high school student was very rare. Usually, boys in high school literary clubs carried around Sin Kyung-lim or Kim Ji-ha, and girls mostly Kang Un-gyo. Some girls liked to read poetry by Lee Hae-in or other poets too embarrassing even to mention. No high school students read Choi Seung-ja. Students our age considered Choi Seung-ja's poetry to be commonplace, too simple, but that was a mistake. In saying this, I don't mean that I understood Choi Seung-ja perfectly, but I also don't believe that the other students understood well the poetry books that they carried around at that time.

"What? What I wrote is all in the style of Choi Seung-ja? Has your extra cramming made you crazy?"

I just smiled. Perhaps, as in many Korean movies, I could have elegantly slapped her cheek at that moment, but Eun-sun was always like that. As for slapping a woman's cheek in the daytime, the music that had been playing for some time was simply too beautiful for that.

"The music is driving me crazy," I told her. "That song's making me crazy for your body."

We were in a rather dark, subterranean tearoom where most of the customers appeared to be students in high school or university, and loud, earsplitting rock music was playing vibrantly. Most of the music was by Ted Nugent, Blue Öyster Cult, or The Edgar Winter Group, all classic rock.

"Let's go," I suggested. "This crammer will buy you dinner."

Some time before, in a novel serialized in a newspaper, I had read the expression "white like a gourd flower" to describe the pale skin on a woman's thigh or breast or hip, I don't remember which. One evening last December, right after the university entrance exam, I discovered that the expression was quite accurate. Eun-sun's naked body gleamed white like a gourd flower under the bed covers. Her body was so white, it seemed almost blue, as if touching her would leave fingerprints.

"Wait," she said, "I have something to ask."

Having taken my clothes off and crawled under the covers, I was hugging Eun-sun's slender body. Not having spoken a single word since entering the hotel, she now began to speak.

"Have you ever slept with a woman?"

As if to draw on her with my fingertip, I touched her full lips with my index finger.

"Never."

But I was lying. In the twelfth grade, I had once visited a prostitute, accompanying an older boy from my school's literary club who had already graduated. For the first time, I had my clothes taken off by a woman other than my mother, and when this woman over thirty stretched a condom with practiced hands onto my private parts, it fell, helpless.

"No, sorry, I lied," I confessed, admitting my visit to the prostitute.

Eun-sun laughed.

"Everyone had ten minutes," I told her. "Yet, my penis, completely covered by a condom, wouldn't stiffen even though the time was almost up. I was still trying hard when my older friend knocked on the door."

"That's all?"

"Yes. Except that I then rushed to the bathroom and masturbated."

Eun-sun laughed for a long time, biting the coverlet with her teeth, then she called me, opening her arms.

"Come here, Adam. You are my first man."

That day, we became adults. Eun-sun and I had already long promised each other we'd become adults on the day of the university entrance exam. That was something everybody did, as ordinary as peeing, something anybody could do. After we had lain naked and hugged each other for a long time, Eun-sun spoke, wiping between her legs with tissues.

"From now on, I will call you Adam."

I felt sorry that I could not call her Eve, and I watched as she tossed all the red-stained tissues into the trash.

"Finally," she said, "I feel finished with the exam. Until coming here and getting this done, I actually felt as though I were still in the middle of the exam."

Our sexual desires had been suppressed all the way through to that hell of a university entrance exam. We had to spend our teens, a time when sexual desire grows most, supervised by teachers. They manipulated us, promising that a moment of abstinence would guarantee success on the exam. Their carrot-and-stick control over our interest in the other sex was part of an insidious strategy to make us model citizens for the future. Five-year-old kindergartners probably enjoyed more sexual freedom than we did. At least they could play doctor.

"I felt like a menopausal woman until sleeping with you. I couldn't feel any desire. Really. Women who survived the

Auschwitz death camp swear that they didn't menstruate while they were there. It's also a miracle for a Korean girl in the twelfth grade to menstruate."

"Yes, I noticed it, too. The boys my age who didn't go to high school had freer, more flexible attitudes toward sex."

Eun-sun and I must, perhaps, have felt the unfairness. In the month between the day of the exam and the day the results were announced, we slept with each other at least once a week, sometimes as often as every third day.

"Do you remember that poem we spent all night writing after we first slept together?" I asked.

Emerging from the tearoom where Mick Jagger was singing "Wild Horses" as loudly as if he were trying to rip out our eardrums, we headed straight to a hotel. Although I had wanted to invite her for dinner to belatedly congratulate her on her success, Eun-sun had refused my invitation, excusing herself because her family was going to have dinner together downtown. After entering the room and locking the door, I had taken Eun-sun in my arms and laid her down on the floor brusquely and quickly, rushing to satisfy my hunger for her.

"Yes, I remember," she replied.

My naked back to the ceiling, I lay prone on top of her, roughly trying to catch my breath. In my mind, I was watching a slow-motion video on rewind of Eun-sun's body, which had clung to me moaning so loudly only moments before. She had moaned and cried out more loudly than any of the rock singers that we had heard in the tearoom. I knew that she was going to leave me.

"Can you recite it, that poem 'December'?" I asked.

On exam day, we each lied to our parents that we were going to the sea with friends to cool our heads, then we sneaked into a hotel room instead where Eun-sun and I lay naked all night composing our poem. Titled "December," it was significant for three reasons. First, it was our earliest joint writing effort. Second, it was the first poem that we wrote after becoming adults. Third, because it implicitly commented on Korea's recent presidential election, it was a meaningful work for both of us.

"Yes," she replied.

"Would you like to read it together?" I asked.

The traffic sounds of buses and motorbikes seeped in through the window. Taking turns, we read one stanza after another:

> We can trust nobody.
> Nobody.
> Nobody.
> Nobody!
>
> I only trust those who have died young.
> I only trust those who have gone crazy on drugs.
> For example,
> I only trust those with names beginning with 'J.'
> Jimi Hendrix, Janis Joplin, Jim Morrison.
> Only those frightful singers.
>
> Dying early
> Or taking drugs,
> In this world,
> Both are possible.
> Even doing both at the same time
> Wouldn't cause any gossip.
>
> That alone is the truth.
> That alone.

Outside the window, the sky was dark. After having sex and reading our poem, we seemed to have nothing more to do, nothing else to talk about. I wondered if smoking at such a moment might not be useful. The silence felt burdensome.

"What are you going to do in the university?" I asked Eun-sun, who was lying beside me, her eyes closed.

"Initially, because nobody will be ordering me to study, there will be nothing to do," she replied. Then, after sitting up and rummaging under the cover with her hands, she added, "I'll learn to drink and smoke. And I'll date. If not, I might become a protester who makes Molotov cocktails."

Eun-sun pulled on her panties after finding them beneath the covers, retrieved her bra from under the pillow where she had placed it and put it on, then pulled her skirt up and drew her sweater back on.

"It's a pity that you failed the exam," she offered. "But I don't have any sympathy for you. To cram for another year so you can go to that first-class university is being greedy. Still, I hope that your greed is fulfilled."

If I had not chosen to cram for another year and had been satisfied with any university that would accept my score, I might have been able to go to the English department at her university on a scholarship.

Eun-sun herself had been telling me things like this since the twelfth grade: "Don't set too high a goal, like going to first-rate university and studying in a first-rate department. It's more sensible to be willing to attend any university that will offer you a scholarship. Besides, a university is just a place to get a certificate for being accepted. The difficult cases are those people who get admitted neither to an exclusive, first-rate university nor to a second-rate university on a scholarship."

Perhaps she was angry at me. I could have gone to the same university as her to study English literature if I hadn't decided to cram for another year.

"Tomorrow is commencement day. That's why my father is

buying me dinner. So, I'll see you again."

Still lying down on my belly, I saw Eun-sun off with my eyes as she went out the door. The loud rock music that I had heard during the day raged through my brain like a high fever. I muttered a few words to myself, without meaning much by them: "Dying early or taking drugs, in this world, both are possible."

After repeating this several times, I realized that these words were verses from our poem, and I had the feeling that they were very much in the style of Choi Seung-ja. No surprise for a poem composed with Eun-sun. I couldn't stop myself from bursting into laughter.

"We can trust nobody. Nobody. Nobody. Nobody!"

In the winter of that year, with the whole nation in uproar over the presidential election, we had held a mock election several times a day with good friends, or with groups in class, or with the whole class, even against the wishes of the teachers. For us twelfth graders, it was impossible to understand why two candidates from the opposition party, who had fought so tenaciously for democracy, could not decide unanimously on one presidential candidate but, instead, had eventually chosen to run separately for election. They were brutes. If I had the right to vote, I would not have voted for anyone. I would have written "Eat country pie, you bastards!" on the ballot slip. It wasn't just me. Our entire generation, which, with the sensitivity of puberty, had witnessed the overthrow of truth through dirty political profiteering, would one day produce vast numbers of people uninterested in politics. I remember receiving a brief letter from my older brother about a week before the election. He had written on a beige-colored postcard as follows:

> "I am trying to sneak out of this country before the election starts. Here, there is nothing more to look for. There is nobody to rely upon. Nobody!"

But my brother, grasping for hope like a drowning man clinging to a piece of straw, supported one of the candidates and had worked at the head of the election campaign for him, as I'd heard. He put himself, so to speak, on the side of "critical support," one of the new phrases coined during the 1987 presidential election. On the evening after the election results were announced, my brother returned home, totally exhausted after going for days without sleep.

"Now, I will leave this country, utterly give it up. I want to be totally immersed in my studies, mind and body. Only sons of bitches live in this country."

I wanted to refute him somehow. Not to defend my country, but myself, as someone who would continue to live there.

"I am not sure any foreign country would make you feel better."

"I know that wherever I go, things won't change much. Could any country be better? They're all made by humans. But . . . but I say, some people can endure hot things better than cold things, while others can endure cold things better than hot. And some people feel better suffering the single stab of a sword to enduring their skin pricked in a close pattern by a needle, while other people feel better having their skin repeatedly pricked to being stabbed once. Let me put it another way. Humans prefer to choose their hell if they're going to have to suffer in it. Do you understand? I am trying to go someplace where my constitution can endure things even slightly more easily."

That night my brother talked to me from the time I returned home from school until eleven o'clock. He then fell into a deep sleep and, as if having a nightmare, he sweated drops like rain, at one point shouting out these meaningless words: "We can trust nobody. Nobody. Nobody. Nobody!"

The next day, my brother went back to Seoul, and I didn't hear from him even after the turn of the year. But then, a few days before I withdrew from the cram school, he came back home only to go away again. Finished with preparations for studying abroad, he was supposed to get on a plane the next day.

"I'm going abroad to study on a scholarship. The plane fare is also being provided by the university there."

My brother was such a person. Aside from the one year of cramming for another exam, he never burdened my mother, nor did he ask her to pay for his university tuition. From his first year until the end of his graduate studies, he got all *A*s. My brother was such a beast.

"I might not come back," he told me. "Whether I marry a white woman or whoever, I will use any and all means to stay in America. But I don't feel comfortable about just leaving all of the burden on your shoulders and fleeing."

My brother was a perfect egoist who could achieve anything that he wanted. A few years before, when he had received his delayed military notice for a physical examination, he was already saying similar things. He said that he would never be forced into the military and would avoid it by all means necessary. He was also a perfect narcissist, constantly looking for the mirror that would reflect his own ability.

"My original plan was to finish graduate school and get a job to support Mother. I was also going to support you for your university tuition. I'm sorry."

I could understand my brother well. Since our elementary school years, when we had eaten our rice only with soy sauce, he had wanted to run away from this country. But the image of my brother studying in America on a scholarship and our mother ringing a handbell to pick up trash in the underground shopping area didn't gel in my mind. He might never have seen Mother underground wiping toilet floors with a cleaning cloth on a stick.

"The field I want to study is only in its early stages in our country," he said. "If I want to study it more comprehensively, I have to go to America."

I wished my brother would stop talking. There was no reason for him to make excuses for himself, even by talking about his studies.

"So far, in college and graduate school, I've studied classical economic theories and international trade, but what I want to study in the future is information theory. It's quite simple. Until now, for the concept of the economy, one has talked about how much thread is used or how many suits can be made using how many yards of cloth, and so on. But from now on, if the taste of the final consumer is not considered, the real value of a product cannot be measured. Ultimately, what remains is the information value, and that's what determines the value of a product."

Although I was nodding my head, absent-mindedly listening to my brother, my brain was getting so filled with complicated stuff that it felt ready to explode. An old incident from my brother's year of cramming came back to me. One day when I came home from school, a maternal uncle who seldom visited us was there.

"I know your stubbornness very well, Elder Sister. And I know also that Jae-hyung is very intelligent. But you did all that you could do. In family circumstances like yours, a parent's duty stops when a child finishes high school."

My mother, who was then pulling a street cart as a food vendor, was cleaning some vegetables for dinner while listening to my uncle. He seemed to have had a drink somewhere before he came, for his face was flushed and his voice quite high-pitched.

"You should now think of your own health. Let's imagine he crams for another year and gets into Seoul National University. Then what?"

My mother was quiet, offering no response, just peeling onions and garlic more swiftly to prepare some food. My uncle, impatient with my mother's attitude, lit a cigarette and began smoking.

"If you entrusted him to me, you and Jae-hyung wouldn't have to suffer, so why are you so stubborn? He can learn to run a business for two or three years, and if he then wants to start his own business, he can do it, becoming his own boss, so why do you oppose it?"

My uncle was a seller who gathered up all kinds of dumped goods and sold them from the back of a loaded Titan Truck at the countryside markets. My mother turned to my uncle whenever she needed some help, so she owed him some money, and for some time already, my uncle had been keeping an eye on my brother. He would always try to persuade my brother, half seriously and half jokingly, to learn about business under him as soon as he graduated high school. Maybe that's why my brother hated him as if he were a viper and ran away whenever he saw Uncle during the three years of high school.

My mother's answer, as always, was firm. "No. I will send Jae-hyung to a university through some means or other. If you're going to talk like that, don't come to see me again."

Now that my brother is going away to study abroad, my mother's ears will again be itching. Relatives and neighbors will be laughing at her behind her back, saying that it is useless to support a child's studies by cleaning public toilets. My brother must have thought that I was interested in what he was talking about, so he continued to explain.

"The area that will be affected the most through the development of information technology is the so-called third sector, and this third sector doesn't deal directly with produced goods but with something intangible, and so, one can say, with information. For example, commercial business, banking, real estate, service industries, among others, and in a broader sense, even technology, all belong to this sector. Resulting from all this, the whole structure of industry will change. In other words, what has been produced so far through the first and second sectors were goods. In the future, however, the third sector will dominate and decide the production of the second sector, and influence that of the first sector, too."

My brother explained the highly developed information society, but what did it have to do with our family's hard life?

"During the 17th and 18th centuries, for the most part," he continued, "raw materials were the most important thing. And during the 18th and 19th centuries, energy was the most important thing. But, since entering the 20th century, the concept of information has become very important. Information will become very powerful, changing future politics, economics, and cultural patterns from the ground up. Whoever holds and controls information will rule the world."

Was it really true, as my brother claimed, that the technology of managing enormous quantities of information combined with the system of quick information processing would contribute to peace for mankind and, what's more, even save the world? How could we believe it? The fact that children in Ethiopia are starving has been publicized throughout the media in great detail, repeatedly emphasized. Yet, had the problem of their starvation been solved? I have not yet heard any news that they have enough to eat. My brother, however, continued.

"The information society even changes people's consciousness. For example, people who are already established, because they belong to the older generation, cannot escape from a material way of thinking, considering fashions or modes as only temporary and superficial, but young people today are more interested in the invisible information values of fashions rather than in the original function of clothing, which is to cover the naked body. Such a change of consciousness, revealed in the change of values from the material-centered to the information-centered, contributes to the generation gap."

My brother flew to America on Korean Air Lines. Maybe, as he said, he might never return to this country. He probably won't. Or perhaps, he might come back to this part of the world. He might occupy a position in a government administration office, after learning about American political science and economics as models for the information society. Or maybe he might return after joining the CIA, the perfect example of a high-information enterprise, one could say.

I began to feel my evenings after cram school had been wasted and thrown away, that I was making poor use of my unprecedented freedom, and I grew bored. A few days after my brother left to study abroad, I stopped going to the cram school. It didn't mean that I had any alternative or some special plan. Every morning, I lied to my mother, pretending to head for the cram school with my lunch box but going to the magazine room in the city library to devour various kinds of printed matter, from women's magazines full of ads for underwear to monthly news magazines revealing the entangled hidden stories behind the Korean coup d'état of December 12, 1979. In this way, the morning hours passed, and in the afternoon, I killed time reading light novels.

Occasionally, I met some high school friends there who were cramming for another year or saw a senior who had been cramming for the third year. Noticing the novels in my hand, they showed some serious concern, but I didn't care. Usually, starting around one or two o'clock, I could finish a close reading of any Korean novel within five hours. Around six or seven o'clock, I'd get up from my chair and wander through town for the evening, but I didn't go down into the city's underground shopping area, so as to avoid my mother.

Using the money that was meant to pay for my cram school fees, I was never hard up for cash. I didn't think about what was coming after nine months. During that time, my life felt worthless.

I would drink beer with friends, but I hadn't learned to smoke. One day, I had such an intense desire for sex that I called Eun-sun. This was in April, when the cherry blossoms were bursting from their buds.

"Hey, Adam, I know that you're not that type of guy, but you don't think that I belong to you because you took my virginity, do you? I may have given you my virginity, but I've never considered offering you my pure love."

When I admitted that I wanted to sleep with her, Eun-sun responded very sharply, so I tried to explain. "No, not that," I said. "I just called wondering if you might also want to enjoy it again after such a long time."

"You're cramming for another year because you want to go to a better university, so why can't I enjoy my own university life? Don't call me for a while. I don't want us to see each other for some time."

That day, I drank several glasses of *soju*. I felt miserable, like when I was sent away by the prostitute because my penis wouldn't get hard despite my ten minutes of effort. But if love wasn't the issue, a person's sex drive could easily be satisfied through masturbation. I only needed to head off to the bathroom after tearing out some revealing photos from magazines in the library.

When I first stopped going to the cram school, the extra time and freedom so wearied me that I had difficulty coping, but after a while, a routine developed naturally. I spent mornings and afternoons reading books in the library, but around seven in the evening, I left and wandered around, looking at the flashing neon signs and movie posters that lined the streets.

Despite walking about aimlessly, my wandering always led automatically to a shop that specialized in selling imported audio goods. The shop, located on the corner of a downtown street, was a small one of only about 12 or 15 square meters, and in the window, a couple of new items as tiny and cute as women's underwear were always being displayed. Just to look at these every evening made my heart race, and in my excitement, I would rush to the same bookstore every day to find and page through audio magazines for the new month. For reasons I don't know, the librarian in charge of journals didn't order any magazines on audio goods, so I would always try to find information about the audio shop's new, displayed products in the bookstore's magazines. While I was doing this, there were often some gentle-looking boys standing around talking trash and looking at car magazines.

"As for sports cars, the Italian Ferrari, the German Porsche, and the English Lotus are the best. The rest are useless."

"Lancias are high class cars, too."

"Look. Here are some pictures from the Turin International Auto Show."

"Who do you think is the fastest race car driver in the world?"

Sometimes, after gazing enthralled at the audio goods in the shop window, I would go to a club on the upper floor of a building where a high school friend of mine worked as a bouncer. There, I would either assist him with bouncing or seat myself at a table near the dance floor and absentmindedly watch the crowd dance. My mother would think that I was studying hard in the reading room.

It was on May 5th, Children's Day, that I first met Hyun-jae. The club was packed, so I had to share a table with her. She was wearing big glasses and sitting across from me at the table in a manner that I hated.

Whenever I saw people listening to a Walkman, I felt an urge to take the earphones from their ears. Anyone listening to a Walkman seemed to me to be a person suffering from emotional insecurity or low intelligence. Not only did she have a Walkman, she went a step further by reading a book in such a loud place with flashing lights. Making the snap judgment that she must be psychotic, I sat down and vaguely watched the stage.

Hyun-jae had quite a nice appearance. Her oval face, short imitation-leather skirt, and blue stockings drove the boys crazy. While I was lost in thought watching the dancers, playboys who noticed that I was not with her would come to the table and ask for a dance. Whenever that happened, she would reject their request with a seemingly practiced hand.

As befitted a national holiday, the place was totally crowded the entire day until closing, and she and I continued to share the table. She sometimes raised her head to push her glasses up or glance at the stage or even watch the dancing, but then she'd only drink the Coke placed before her on the table and appeared to have no interest in dancing.

The DJ started to play "Please Don't Go" by KC and The Sunshine Band. For some reason, the DJ always played that song at precisely twenty to eleven. Whenever the slow music started, the playboys came to her asking for a dance, and this time, a very persistent fellow was begging her, almost kneeling in front of her. After looking at his face once and sighing, she took off her earphones, leaving them hanging around her neck and, unfolding her long, entwined legs, stood up. So handsome was the young guy that all a girl could do was sigh.

Although my behavior was rather devious, I was very curious about the book that she was reading, so I stealthily opened it and had to laugh loudly. The book was *Sungmoon Compound English*, something a high school student would use. She didn't give the impression of being a high school student, however, but of a cram student who had failed the university exam.

Even after "Please Don't Go" had finished, she didn't return to her seat. The next song was "Jezebel" by Sade, and the girl seemed not to be coming back before the slow music had ended. I glanced at the clock, then got up so that I wouldn't miss the last bus. Before leaving, I went to the bathroom to wash my face with cold water and relieve myself. I then picked up my bag, which I had left at the ticket office, and was soon in the hall not far from the club's entrance, waiting for the elevator to come up. It seemed that the slow music was over, for loud music was now bursting from the entrance, and loud voices could sometimes be heard.

The elevator soon arrived quietly, and young people poured out, leaving it emptied for me to enter. The elevator man, after waiting briefly for other people, was about to push the close button when some people rushing from the entrance shouted "Stop!" It was a mixed group of girls and boys, some of them playboys, and the girl was also with them. Holding her hand tightly as if afraid to lose her, the guy who had asked her for a dance was laughing and making small talk with his friends. She had her Walkman earphones on again but not her glasses, and was staring at me intently with her small, dark eyes that resembled buttonholes. They reminded me of fragile doll's eyes.

Out of all Munch's paintings, it was *Puberty*, a medium-sized oil painting, that I liked most. I would often stop by the bookstore downtown specializing in imported books to look at the painting. A naked prepubescent girl is sitting blankly on a bed. She is insecure, with breasts not yet fully developed and hiding her pubic region shyly with both hands. This girl, who stares at the viewer so directly, always made my heart beat faster. Whenever I saw the painting, I thought of a little bird shivering in a storm. Puberty and the image of the little bird shivering in a storm seemed to have something in common, or so I felt. In each, there was the mixture of desire and anxiety for a pure world.

When she tapped me on my shoulder one day, I was again looking at the painting.

"Do you like this picture?"

I hated it when women tapped me on the shoulder. Wondering who it was, I turned around and there was a girl, whom I didn't know, smiling shyly at me. It was an embarrassed smile, the sort that appears after calling out to someone in a moment of boldness, as if seeking forgiveness in the uncertainty. The Walkman hanging around her neck suddenly caught my eyes.

"Don't you remember me?" she asked.

"Ah-h-h," I stuttered, my voice breaking, and I nodded that I recognized her. I cannot easily explain it, but I was very glad, as though I were meeting a woman whom I had been wishing to see again. I looked at her, dressed this time in red stockings and a short denim skirt, as if it were her own personal uniform. I showed her the picture that I had been staring at, and then we left the bookstore together. The owner, an old man who had been watching carefully should anyone try to steal a book, buried his face in the newspaper.

"Actually, I followed you in from the street."

She offered this information, unasked, once we were outside.

"Did you?" I said. "I didn't realize. Shall we go to a tearoom?"

Some boys passing by glanced at her legs. I felt good. At my suggestion that we should go to the tearoom, she stopped walking and stared at me intently, with the dreamy look that I had seen before in the elevator.

"I have already surrendered to you," she told me. "I followed you because I like you."

"What do you mean?"

"It means that we don't have to waste time."

We decided to find a hotel.

"Actually," she said, "I know a hotel where we can watch videos all night."

She started walking toward the university area where a lot of hotels were located. Walking together for about half an hour, she and I talked about things selectively, revealing nothing potentially harmful even though we had no intention of seeing each other again after sleeping together.

"Do you often go to that club?" I asked.

"No, I usually go to the one in Hyangchon-dong, but that day

I just wanted to try it out." Her voice was young and clear, like the voice of a princess in an animated film.

"By the way," I asked, "what are you doing with that Walkman plugged in your ears? Studying?"

"Not studying. Listening to music."

She pushed the play button of the Walkman and plugged one earphone into my ear. In very low tones came the voice of Jim Morrison singing "Light My Fire." My guess that she would be listening to trash music like Boy George, Michael Jackson, or Wham! had been completely wrong.

"What a surprise! I didn't imagine you were into the classics."

She really was. When it came to rock music, she was a classicist. She listened only to Jim Morrison, Jimi Hendrix, and Janis Joplin, calling them "the three holy *J*s." Once, I asked Hyun-jae which of the three she most liked.

"Morrison, of course."

"Why?"

"Because he had so many songs banned."

"Didn't Joplin and Hendrix, too?"

"But I don't like blacks," she countered. "Or women. And Morrison is handsome, isn't he? And the son of a navy admiral."

She would also say things like, "Know why I like 'the three holy *J*s'? It's because their music has something arousing in it, which is very sexy. Especially the guitars. The guitar parts, you know, seem to turn me on. Isn't that sexy?"

Thinking back, it seems like music was the main topic of our impassioned conversations. Once, she even told me, "I often stifle a desire to leap from the top of my apartment building by listening to rock music."

After saying this, an expression of misery appeared on her face, as if she had fallen from the 12th floor and struck the ground lightly with her face.

That was later, when I knew her better, but that first time, when I expressed surprise that she listened to Morrison, she asked, "What's so surprising?"

"I thought that you might be listening to Boy George or Michael Jackson."

Understanding exactly what I meant, Hyun-jae twanged, "Oh, yeah."

Then, she added, "You mean people like F. R. David or the Eurythmics?"

"Yes."

"I don't listen to garbage like that," she said. "Music is so corrupt these days."

Turn on the radio, and it's full of neutral music, with sweet voices. Music that makes you puke. There's no spirit in such music. No spirit in music once known as "Rock Spirit" for its rebelliousness and impassioned love.

"This music thrills me. It's so weird, and it makes me cry. Whenever I tire of studying for tests, I listen to Hendrix or Joplin, or Morrison. After about a half hour at high volume, I feel refreshed all over. Actually, I get dehydrated. And because I use earphones, I go deaf. Then, the textbooks I'm reading become the focus of my hatred, like the rotten world that those singers attack in their music. With that feeling, I can study all night without sleep."

She told me that she attacked her textbooks with the same hatred that rock music directed against the world.

"Your hips look nice," I told her.

After entering the hotel, she took off her skirt and turned around. Her straight legs with their slim thighs as firm as well-dried firewood were very impressive. And the fully rounded hips supported by such slender legs were so unbalanced, they almost made me dizzy.

"Hips?"

"Yes, your hips look nice."

"I don't like men who stare at women's hips. A man who says my hips are nice makes me shudder."

"Why?"

"Because the important part of a woman is down there."

"Then should I take back what I said?"

"No, I'll forgive you. In fact, I wanted to hear you say that. Compliments about hips are good to hear, don't you think? It makes me feel erotic."

Hyun-jae was a woman alive only below the waist and in her ears. Whenever she wasn't making love, headphones were stopping up her ears, and whenever she wasn't listening to music, she was getting stopped up between her legs. To understand her, one had to find the connection between music and sex.

"Can I smoke?" she asked.

"Sure."

Hyun-jae lit a cigarette and smoked. The sex had been great. Twice, my hard penis had been inside her. While smoking, she changed the tapes in her Walkman, then she shared the headphones with me, putting one in my ear, the other in her ear. Clearly, there was a connection here. For her, music and sex were one. What, does it mean, though, to be one? After making love, as if we'd just remembered, we finally asked each other's names.

"You weren't bad," she observed. "How many times have you slept with a woman?"

That sort of question bears the fingerprints of a woman. Eun-sun, before having sex for the first time in her life, had shyly asked, "Have you ever slept with a woman?" But that question can bear different fingerprints. Eun-sun asked whether I had or not, whereas Hyun-jae was asking how many times I had. The difference between the two questions, subtly expressed but very different, might measure the difference between Eun-sun and Hyun-jae. Moreover, if one takes into account the difference between asking before sex and asking after sex, how much more of a difference would be measured?

"I don't know how many times," I admitted, "but you're the second woman I've made love to."

"Really? Who was the first girl you slept with?"

I was in trouble. Should I mention that old prostitute from high school or Eun-sun? Who had I first made love to? I didn't love the prostitute enough to say it was her, whereas saying it was Eun-sun would not answer the question accurately. I would be plagued by this troubling question of my first woman for my whole life. O, you, half-fucked woman, forever will you itch in my heart. Please forgive me. I answered without deciding who it was.

"Yeah, there was someone."

Hyun-jae again twanged "Oh, yeah." From the headphone in my left ear, I could hear Jimi Hendrix singing "Can You See Me." I turned my face and looked at her. Hyun-jae was lying flat on her back staring at the ceiling. Her face seemed familiar, as if I had known her before.

"What are you doing?" I asked.

"I'm sad."

A line of tears was flowing down Hyun-jae's right cheek. I thought of the girl in the Munch painting as I wiped away her tears.

"Are you cramming for another year?" I asked.

"No."

"I saw your book, *Sungmoon Compound English*. I'm sorry."

Hyun-jae was not a cram student. She was in the 12th grade of a girls' high school. It was as if I had fallen into a trap, the sort of cheap literary trick often used in bad novels. But if I were writing this as a novel, I wouldn't have chosen to construct such a literary trick. In fact, among the third-rate novels that I was reading in the library, I often noticed such tricks. Stories describing how a male protagonist wakes up "drunk" in a hotel room and discovers a woman lying beside him, perhaps a young student or the wife of his friend, or how a male protagonist sleeps 'passively' with a woman who adores him because she approached him actively and somehow tricked him. Those descriptions are just cheap frauds used by writers to protect the male character. Just like Oedipus, who didn't know what he was doing, so his character was absolved, thereby leaving him innocent.

But I'm not like that. To be frank, I'm the sort of guy who feels like throwing up if I encounter such hypocrisy. I don't blame myself for having slept with a high school girl. On the contrary, I can imagine wishing that all the world's high school girls were my lovers. Besides, I myself had been a high school student only a year earlier.

"How do you think you can go to a university if you live like this?" I asked her.

"I'll do it, some way or other. These days, I've heard that students cramming for another year are exported, so if I fail, I can go abroad to study. Then I can transfer back to a university in Korea."

She told me that the previous summer she had gone to America after being invited by a relative, and that she'd heard that going overseas to study after graduating from high school was easy for those with money. I found out much later that Hyun-jae's father was the owner of a well-known construction company in our province. Once, while standing before a brand-new Korean car at an exhibition, she casually said, "Maybe I should ask my father to buy me a car after the exam. I could drive as fast as I want and then plunge headlong into the sea."

Her father and mother, and her two brothers, who were graduate students, all had their own cars, she told me.

"Isn't it better, though, to attend a university here rather than go abroad like the dregs of a defeated troop that's been forced to run away?"

"I won't be running away like the dregs of a defeated troop," she countered. "Whether I pass or fail the university entrance exam, and no matter what country I end up going to, I'll leave Korea with dignity when I do leave."

"Where will you go?"

"Someplace like Paris or Vienna," she mused. "Sydney might be good, too."

That night, we left the hotel before twelve. Hyun-jae took a taxi and went home first. We didn't make any promises to meet again. On my way home, I whistled a medley of all The Beatles' hit songs. Somehow, I felt that I would see her again because we had wanted to know each other's names and because we had connected through sex and music.

When I arrived home, my mother showed me a letter from my brother and asked me to read it to her. The letter began with "I'm sorry for my delay in writing," and continued:

> Only now do I feel that the nausea from my life in America is slowly settling. Although I had thought that I was well prepared and fully determined, dealing with the immense raw "data" (?) that is America is not easy. I, however, am growing more used to America than other people who have come here to study. Although people claim that it's not the foreignness during the first several months but the loss of self-identity from a long-term stay in a foreign country that is much harder to endure, I didn't think that such a disease (HOMESICKNESS!) would ever infect me. I would like to be completely immersed in my studies for about ten years. You will think that I am an egoist, won't you? But, rather, feel pity (!!) for me because I was banished from my country . . .

When I finished reading, my mother looked disappointed.

My brother had added "How is Mother doing?" at the end of the letter, as if it had been an afterthought, like a PS. Then, in a note labeled as a PS: "As for the books I sent from Seoul, you can do whatever you want with them. Maybe they should just be sold to a ragpicker." The things that my brother most wanted to say were probably included in the PS. In some letters, the PS is the main part, and some people express the things that they most desire to say in the form of a PS.

My brother's PS sounded like a code to me. He seemed to be implying that he'd never come back to Korea. As he himself had said, he wanted to live in America, by any means necessary. If he could not finish a degree, he would get a job regardless of whether it was in a laundry or a carwash, or he would obtain American citizenship by marrying a white woman or hooking up with an old Korean widow. What made him feel banished from his country? What made him put exclamation marks, even two of them, after the word "pity"? Excessive self-pity would be pure self-deceit and self-pride.

It was the beginning of June, and the summer season was starting in earnest. Olympic fever was gradually heating up the whole country. In all kinds of public offices and on the streets, people were counting down to the expected opening day of the Olympic Games, and the news media was airing special programs and reporting on the preparations. But most citizens were just being dragged along. For several years, the 1988 Olympic Games had been constantly advertised, as a form of government-sponsored indoctrination, and the citizens, who were forced to listen to news about the Olympic Games, endured it like a form of irritating pollution. Of course, some people, such as cunning politicians and business people, would be out to make profits.

Hyun-jae and I were growing closer. She would show up stealthily every two days at the club where I was lingering, and sink into a seat at my table. One time, she came to the special bookstore for imported books, where I was looking at Munch's *Puberty* in a book, came up from behind, and covered my eyes with her hands. We didn't make any appointments for where or when to meet, and we didn't need to say that we loved each other. Hyun-jae and I would go off immediately to find a room in a hotel as soon as we saw each other. As though we were making a pilgrimage through all the downtown hotels, we chose a new one every time. When we had finished making love, she would always listen to music, plugging one headphone into my ear or keeping both headphones to herself. She seemed not to be listening to music but trying to crawl into the silence of her own world. Her Japanese Walkman had its own speaker so that one could listen to music without headphones, but Hyun-jae never used the speaker when two people were listening to music.

It's sad not to play music for two people to listen to, so I asked Hyun-jae, "Isn't it uncomfortable using earphones?"

"No, it's fine. Actually, I would feel terrified if I didn't use the headphones. I'd feel myself being cast away in the midst of an immense sea."

"I thought people liked to share good music, or at least let others listen, too."

"There's no need to worry whether or not others can listen to the music," she informed me. "Since I record the music and listen to it repeatedly by myself, I don't need anybody else."

Hyun-jae and I were not getting any closer than that. She was a girl who could not love anybody. She knew nothing of being loved or of loving. One time in a hotel, drinking beer out of cans, we discussed love, pretending to be quite serious.

"Love?" she asked. "Isn't it all just 'give and take'? Give and take each other's body for a short time. Sometimes even the heart, too. But it is like borrowing each other. I would never give my body or my heart completely. When I need to, I will lend them out for a while, then get them back."

The first thing that the old generation teaches young boys and girls in sex education is monogamy. Because it is already established as part of the social system, one learns it automatically, without being programmed for it. But the more sexual experiences that one has as a young teenager, the less effect those lessons on monogamy will have. Young boys and girls who have experienced sex at a young age will never again be satisfied with monogamy. They'll continuously seek new partners for sex. For them, monogamy has nothing of value to offer.

"When was your first experience?" I once asked her.

"I matured a bit early. It was in the 8th grade."

"That's quite early," I observed. "From then on, did you 'give and take'?"

"At the time, it just happened. It started innocently, like children playing doctor, and ended awkwardly. Also, I didn't think much about it. Only from the 9th grade onwards did I start to enjoy having sex. Without it, I would have killed myself."

She told me that she had experienced serious anxiety before her high school entrance exam. Strong pressure in her chest, a headache that seemed to almost split her head, unnerving insecurity, and constant stress were among some of the symptoms.

"I thought that other students were working harder than I was even though I tried my best, studying as hard as I could. I always felt insecure and stressed."

So she gradually learned to enjoy having sex, little by little, like getting high on heroin, or so Hyun-jae told me.

"Have you ever thought that it might be immoral, or a sin?" I asked her. "Have you at least thought about your parents?"

"I've never felt that way. I thought that if I got strong enough, I would be above the sin, as if I were playing a children's game. I had the feeling that I belonged to nobody. This feeling was quite powerful. I don't feel any sorrow for my parents. In fact, in our family, everybody is on their own, so being independent is normal.

Whatever the business, if it's someone else's affair, they deal with it in an official, businesslike way."

The more she talked, the more clearly I could see her inside her head. The words we use are often deceptive even if they're meant to seem honest, but she was speaking very frankly and sincerely. I felt as if I could make out the order not only of her brain but even of the blood vessels in all their complex interconnections.

She wanted a room just for herself, an inner room not shared with anyone that nobody could peer into. She didn't watch TV. Watching TV is a means of enjoyment for people who own a room. TV is the fifth wall only for those who already have four walls. Therefore, since she had no room, she listened to the radio, or to cassette tapes. By that, I mean she listened neither to the endlessly flowing FM music programs nor to the endless copies of tapes. What she listened to came not through her ears but was an inner echo of her loneliness. The radio is a kind of loneliness.

And then what about her use of sex? That was also a pure kind of loneliness. For her, sex was not for love, nor for reproduction. Sex for love and reproduction was already impure sex. What she wanted from sex was an awakening within the moment, an awareness of her own life. The more that one can enjoy, the more easily one can change from one's current self to a different self.

These things are all for self-satisfaction. They allow self-sufficiency. It is egoism, pure and simple. Yes, though I believe that egoism can benefit others, too. But egoism doesn't require the understanding of others. Ultimately, the quest for more self-satisfaction and self-sufficiency won't rescue a person. I knew that she would sacrifice herself for her self alone.

While we made a pilgrimage through the hotels without making any promises and plugged the headphones into our ears after having sex, half of June passed us by. This city in a valley with its short spring and fall and its hot summer and cold winter smelled of dry dust and pungent sweat. On one of those early summer days, I received one of the three things that I most wanted to have when I was nineteen.

"May I sit here?" I heard a voice inquire.

This occurred about an hour after I had sat down at my usual table, absent-mindedly watching the people on the crowded dance floor. As if having already decided to sit regardless of my response, the person casually took the seat next to me before I could answer. A bit irritated, I looked at the person the voice belonged to.

"I didn't want to be rude," the person said, "but I've already acted rudely."

Seated next to me was a woman in her mid-thirties. She had a long neck and very long hair.

"I noticed that you've only been watching the stage. Maybe you don't know how to dance, or don't like to dance, I assume."

Her voice was measured, as if adjusted to a metronome, and her enunciation was precise, as if she were pronouncing every vowel and consonant separately. Intrigued by her voice, I scrutinized the woman and found that not only her neck and hair were long. Her fingers, which I saw at a glance, and her waist, were long as well. She was graceful and beautiful.

"No," I finally said, "I like watching."

"What do you think about when you watch others dance? People say that one must be looking inside when one watches without paying attention."

She didn't wear any makeup. I felt the pure beauty of a middle-aged woman. The fact that she talked to me so informally, without asking first, aroused me.

"I'm staring at my ennui," I told her.

"I need a male model," she said. "I'll pay. Would you like to work for one night?"

I didn't have anything else to do. Because Hyun-jae usually

came on Saturdays and Sundays, I knew that she wouldn't be there that day. She might have been going to a different club on Fridays, I wasn't sure.

"Okay," I agreed.

I followed her. We took the elevator down to the parking lot. She left me standing alone for a little while, then came back driving a red medium-sized car and opened the front passenger door.

"Get in."

The car was filled with CityJazz cassettes that bore the label "Windham Hill."

"I need a new, young model."

When I asked if she was an artist, she didn't respond. She just pulled out a cigarette with her free hand, put it between her lips, and offered one to me. I shook my head, and she lit her cigarette. I had seen Hyun-jae smoking several times, but whenever she smoked, she looked as if she was just playing with fire, which seemed simultaneously funny and risqué, but the way that this woman took out and smoked a cigarette made me feel lightheaded, as if I were drinking beer. The drive didn't last very long. She stopped in the middle of an alley, a hidden place that one wouldn't expect in the middle of town.

With her key, she opened a small iron gate between the walls. Behind the gate, there was a short alley, and after that a spacious studio. Entering the place, I felt the strong smell of oil paints assail my nose. In the room, which was about 66 square meters, some dusty canvases and drawing instruments lay spread all over. A few sofas and a bed, as well as a sink, were on one side of the room.

"Would you like a cup of coffee?"

"Sure."

While she was making coffee, I looked at some of the sketches and oil paintings lying around. They all showed a woman's mouth performing fellatio on the genitals of a half-obscured man. Those images, painted or drawn from the perspective of the man, who was standing with his genitals in the woman's mouth, were painted in the simple primary colors of animated films, and some had speech bubbles near the woman's mouth saying, "Oh! Great!"—as if cut and pasted from a comic book. The text didn't make the images obscene; rather, the images were made normal and humorous, as if they were nothing special.

"Should I put on some music?" she asked, bringing over the coffee. "What kind of music do you like?"

"Do you have Ben E. King or B.B. King? The Doors or The Animals are also okay."

She rummaged in several boxes stuffed with records.

"So," she observed. "Your taste is quite standard. Anything else?"

"Early Rolling Stones or early Rod Stewart."

She opened the cover of the turntable and put on CCR, Creedence Clearwater Revival. Apparently, in Chinese, their name means "a band of clear water." Like a captivating story recounted by old people from olden times, "Bad Mood Rising" played. Was a bad moon rising? Outside, the sky was heavily overcast.

"You are rebellious, aren't you?" she remarked. "Nowadays, the suffix 'post' is popular everywhere. Post-Modernism, Post-Classicism, Post-Industrial Society, Post-Marxism, Post-Sexism."

I looked around at the pictures strewn about her room. Were those considered Post-Sexism? They seemed like pop art to me.

"Post-Sexism? Like these paintings?"

She laughed out loud at my question. Not the forced laughter from watching a comedian get drenched with water or hit in the face with a pie, but real laughter, that comes from laughing at something truly funny.

"Post-Sexism?" she said. "I just made that one up. Of course, for all we know, people might be talking about such things in New York or Munich."

I laughed with her. Drinking coffee, we talked a bit more about music.

"You must enjoy 'oldies but goodies,'" she said.

"Yes. Without them, the world would quickly fall apart."

"You mean," she asked, "that they act as a brake on our accelerated world?"

At the time, I didn't understand what the expression "accelerated world" meant. She thought for a while, supporting her chin in her hand. Then, she explained the expression in the simplest way she could.

"It could also be called *fascist* speed, and it reveals the mechanism by which our current industrial society races forward at a frightening rate, propelled by various institutions and vast amounts of capital. For example, take a car company run by a family-owned conglomerate. As soon as it makes a new product, the business continuously promotes it through the media—a so-called neutral, official institution."

"I'm sorry to interrupt you," I said, "but how is the media neutral?"

"Oh, the modes of transmission, I mean. The technical instruments are neutral. Let's assume that there's a gun. It can be used by a burglar or a policeman. Do you see what I mean? In this sense, even the media is neutral."

I nodded, showing that I understood. She continued to talk about advertising.

"The brains of people today have been severely damaged by the endless blows of advertising from childhood to adulthood, so they buy products almost as a conditioned reflex, without resistance or defense. And very soon, before the new car has even replaced its first sparkplug, the automobile company begins advertising a new car with a slightly different body or door shape, and the consumer will buy the newly advertised car, selling his own, still usable car. What happens then? The earth created from such an accelerated world will eventually become a junkyard, won't it? An enormous grave for cars."

"I understand you better now," I said. "One could call such a world an 'accelerated world' in which speed is the most important value and only going forward is accepted as development and success."

While the automotive industry will gradually transform the Earth into a car dump, the arms industry, which is even bigger, might quickly bring about the world's end. To maintain an industry that has become monstrously big and out of control, and to increase profits for the country, arms companies and the government either have to produce ever-new armaments and sell them to other countries or stir up local wars to create demand. More research funds will be spent developing new weapons, and the weapons developed by investing huge amounts of money and talent will, of course, become more fatal and precise. In Europe and Asia, old missiles are being replaced by newly developed ones almost yearly. Anyone with enough money can purchase a small rocket launcher. It doesn't matter if the person is a gangster or insane.

The song had changed. "Sweet Hitch-Hiker" was playing.

"You seem to dislike contemporary bands," she noted. "Do you have a reason?"

"They lack soul."

"Soul!" she exclaimed, and clapped her hands. "That's exactly right. What singers these days do best is shake their pelvis. They all wear black sunglasses. Like sissy boys, they moan like the sex-obsessed. Like this."

She moaned loudly: "Aaah, aaah."

"In the old days," she added, "you could see real shows. Even in Korea, there were real rock bands in the sixties. I was in my twenties then. There were real bands like ADD4, He 6, and the Key Boys. They were far better than the trash bands these days. Their strength was live performance. Back then, if people wanted to play music, they had to do it on an American military base, but that meant that they had to pass an audition in front of the Americans. To do that, a band had to be really good."

She lit another cigarette. If she was in her twenties during the sixties, she must be in her forties now. But she looked to be in her mid-thirties or even in her early thirties.

"At that time," she continued," there was even a band in Seoul called the Devils. As they sang, they dragged coffins around onstage. They really put on a show. They were very active. These days, everything is just fake, a puppet theater."

We finished our coffee and started work. As she requested, I took my clothes off and sat down on a chair in the middle of the room. With nothing on, I sat and listened to "Midnight Special," then to "Susie Q." She started to work only after setting up the paints and her drawing tools.

"Your body has good balance. I knew that my eyes were accurate."

Gazing intensely at my crotch, she began sketching with her pencil, drawing the area between my legs. My penis, only slightly erect when I had taken off my clothes, now began to grow bigger, utterly undaunted. I glanced at the clock, which showed that it was nearly eleven. Then, noticing that my penis was becoming ever more erect, I felt my face flush with embarrassment.

"I'm sorry," I apologized. "I can't do anything to stop it."

She laughed and assured me, "That's okay. This is the condition that I want you in."

She got up from her seat and approached me, correcting my posture. As her warm hand touched the area between my legs, I couldn't endure it any longer and hugged her waist. For a moment, she held my penis tightly.

"Listen," I said, "this is just a ruse, isn't it? So why don't we just have sex right now?"

She acted upset. With a mocking smile, she said, "You little boy. You're confused about this work, thinking it's foreplay, just pseudo-art."

She released my penis and returned to her place to continue working. Some time had passed since CCR had stopped playing. As if presaging heavy rain, a cool wind had been rattling the window for some time.

"I can draw a man's penis with my eyes closed," she said. "I don't need a man's body, just inspiration. I'm trying to get an image from you."

"By touching and sucking, you mean?"

She got really upset, kicked the easel over, and strode toward me. "Impudent model!"

We fell onto each other, getting entangled on the floor, and stroked each other's bodies, licking with our tongues. For the first time I experienced foreplay, extended foreplay. In previous sexual experiences, there had been no foreplay prior to intercourse. Not used to the slowly increasing tension, I tried to hurry, speeding up, but again and again, she forced me to break off. Our very intensive foreplay soon brought me to a climax.

"Go to the bed," she told me.

As I was crawling into the bed, she rummaged around in a drawer and found a diaphragm, which she slipped in. She then took a cassette for the player. Gordon Lightfoot began singing "If You Could Read My Mind."

Stretched out, her legs were very long. As if I were driving up the Gyeongbu Expressway for a long time, I nibbled at her from the top of her foot to the split between her legs. She stroked my hair with her hands, making groaning sounds. After a while, I found and opened her, and she accepted me deep inside her.

She held my waist tightly with her long legs, and we played

like a horse with two heads. In the climax of pleasure, our sleepless night deepened. By the time that Janis Joplin's "Me and Bobby McGee" was playing on the cassette of oldies but goodies, we were lying on the bed hugging each other's waists. She moved her body a little and lit a cigarette.

"A shaman lady is singing," she observed.

Outside raindrops were falling: *todok*, *todok*.

While we were listening to the song, someone outside began knocking on the window. Without moving to get up, she kept blowing cigarette smoke up in the air. The person knocking at the window called in a low voice.

"Older Sister, Older Sister, please open the door."

She still didn't move, just put her finger to my lips, indicating that I shouldn't utter a word.

"Older Sister, it's us. Don't you remember us?"

This voice was different, but both were voices belonging to boys not quite past puberty. She left her cigarette in my charge and, wrapping herself with the blanket, got up to approach the window.

"Go home," she told them. "My lover is here."

The night again became quiet outside, and I thought it rather strange that they went away without the least resistance. She walked to the bedside and retrieved her cigarette.

"Regardless of whether they're old or young," she said, "men believe that they can do anything they want with a woman after embracing her once. Korean men—I'm really sick of them."

She climbed onto the bed and touched my hair, and I asked her, "Why did they leave without any protest?"

"Oh, before I sleep with men, I always tell them that my lover is a Taekwondo master. That's the method that I used overseas."

She put her mouth to my nipples and sucked on them as she stretched her long arm below, sliding it down to take my soft penis in her hand and make it erect again. The sound of the rain grew louder.

"A very long time ago," she said, "I left Korea. First, I went to Paris and then to Munich. After that, I traveled between Munich and New York, all the while suffering from a complex over being Asian, cursing whites. At the same time, I tried to be cosmopolitan and worried whenever I saw an Asian, wondering if the person was Korean. Of course, I had some very good Korean friends I would have died for, but I stuck closely to them, and had no contact with other Koreans."

Her manner of enunciating words, expressing them as if according to a metronome, was that of an elementary school child. Like that of inarticulate individuals who have long lost their mother tongue.

"Nothing went well," she admitted, "neither painting nor life, so I thought of home. But someday, I will return to the West. Korea is not the place for me to succeed. Even if I fail, it won't be in this place."

We drank beer, took showers, ate beef cooked over a grill, and made love again. We listened to music, changing cassettes, and I repeatedly attempted, for the first time, to slowly release cigarette smoke after holding it in my mouth.

"Do you believe in love?" she asked me. "Judging from the expression in your eyes and from your musical taste, you would seem to."

"Love cannot solve all the problems in the world," I told her, "but it can solve some. Love can be an antiseptic in a rotten world."

"Bread still goes bad despite the preservatives," she said. "Love is also corrupt. In a world without love, only sex can replace it."

As our heads lay on our pillows, I observed from close up that there were fine, layered wrinkles around her eyes. I wanted to ask what would then replace corrupt sex. And if we were to reverse the corrupt sex, couldn't love then appear? Therefore, the cause of all the world's sins and corruption is the corruption of love, and the solution would be love, the cause? But that would be too conceptual, too much like a game of circular logic.

Close to dawn, we finally fell asleep. After turning off the lights, the room fell into pitch-blackness, making the light on the cassette player's power button—still on after the cassette had finished playing—shine red like a lit cigarette. I drifted into a colorless sleep without dreams.

The next day, she got up first and put a cassette in the player after rummaging inside a big bamboo basket. Outside, the rain continued. On a morning after one has slept overnight in a friend's house, the falling rain outside, heard while still lying in bed, can sound so beautiful that it refreshes all feelings. We experience such a good rain only a few times in an entire life. To enjoy the springiness of the bed, I rolled myself over with all the strength in my body. The bedsprings groaned, then made a low squeaking sound: *squee-gee, squee-gee*. She had left her lower parts bare, wearing only a large T-shirt, and was standing in front of the gas cooker, showing off legs fine enough for a panty hose ad.

"You look so cool," I said. "I'd like to introduce you to the Namyoung nylon company."

"What does Namyoung nylon do?"

"It's a company that produces panty hose."

"It's not polite to ridicule an older person early in the morning," she scolded. "If you're awake, would you like to help me cook?"

Unlike her, I put on only trousers without a shirt. Then I went to the sink, where I washed my face roughly with the purified water before stepping beside her.

"How can I help you?" I asked.

"Oh, it's easy. Just hug me from behind until I finish toasting the bread and making salad."

I opened my arms and embraced her gently from behind, my hands softly covering her breasts like a bra.

"Is this good enough?" I asked. "Don't you need any other help from me?"

"Could you tell me some stories until I finish? It doesn't matter what."

"What kind of story should I tell you?"

"Any kind. Really, anything is fine. Or you can tell me how I was last night."

"I would rather tell you how you look this morning."

The savory smell of bread toasting filled the air while the water boiling for coffee steamed with a *shik-shik* sound. She took two steps left to open the refrigerator, taking out fruits and vegetables, then four steps right to start making a salad at the sink. Hugging her from behind, I accompanied her every move, as if borne on her back.

"When I'd opened my eyes fully," I began, "you were standing in front of the stove. You were wearing only a shirt, revealing your hips and your body gave off its scent as you made breakfast. From behind, you looked beautiful, and your back, in its breadth, looked lonely and empty. You are working at preparing a very tasty meal now. We are going to eat it."

I was stuttering a bit in my effort.

"Is that all?" she asked.

"No."

I realized that the story I was telling her was similar to the half-page story "Women When They Put Their Clothes on in the Morning," by Richard Brautigan.

But the reason for my stuttering was not only that I felt sorry for paraphrasing someone else's short story while hugging her from behind, so I explained about Brautigan.

"Oh, it's like a beautiful poem?"

"No. It's dirty prose," I said.

She sighed deeply, and we sat on the sofa half naked, eating from two big plates, both of us holding one each. We didn't talk.

Only once, she tried to make me laugh.

"Should I tell you a story?" she began. "Long ago, in a village in China, there lived seven wise men, and they went off to sea one day, sailing on a big plate."

After telling that much, she closed her mouth for a few seconds and drew a line with her index finger around the edge of the plate she was holding.

"If the plate had been bigger," she then said, "this story would have gone on longer."

She offered to give me a ride home, but I declined, saying that I didn't want her to put on her clothes. Although I didn't say so, I wouldn't have felt right about arriving at my place in her car. Also, the silence that might settle between us when we had to wait for a traffic light would be burdensome. She tried to pay me for the work, but I told her that it wasn't necessary.

"Don't make me a male prostitute."

"But, I want to offer you something."

"If you really want to," I said, "then give me a book of art prints . . . if you have one of Munch's."

After rummaging in a paper box, which had obviously been put away for a long time, she found a Japanese book with Munch's prints. It was one from the publishing company that I saw in the imported books bookstore that I sometimes visited.

"Thank you. This is exactly what I've wanted for a long time."

I turned and walked away after saying goodbye. A few steps later, I heard her call out: "You'll think of me as a strange woman, won't you?"

"No. I don't know. Maybe."

"A free person is one who can acknowledge other people's lifestyles and ways of thinking."

I went out of the alley. Once out of the short, narrow alley, I was immediately in the center of the town again. I thought about freedom. The freedom that she had insisted upon captivated me and made me reflect.

Asking someone to unconditionally acknowledge other lifestyles and ways of thinking is pure self-centeredness, for it's just a means of demanding that as I do to you, you should unconditionally do to me, by acknowledging my lifestyle and my way of thinking. But those who unconditionally acknowledge and show understanding for other people's lifestyles and ways of thinking become irresponsible and less strict with themselves in the end.

Desiring more and greater freedom makes people lose their sense of reality. Trying to expand human freedom beyond one's reason and the world that one lives in brings the loss of reality, or even of the things called truth and paradise. In art, such freedom expresses itself as kitsch. In a world without reality, the real world cannot possibly be revealed, and the world just as it stands becomes the object of play.

Like those pictures hanging on the walls of barber shops in Korea depicting some deep-forest scene with a vagabond in a bamboo hat or some country village with a watermill, kitsch of the 19th century was a kind of self-monologue expressing self-nostalgia with no distance between self and object, whereas kitsch of the 20th century treats visions playfully and freely, reflecting upon them from a distance. The former would be called representative, and the latter abstract. If there is not only 'sweet' kitsch but also 'sour' kitsch, as Hermann Broch suggested, then 19th-century kitsch is sweet, but 20th-century kitsch is sour.

Even now, I clearly remember the picture that I saw in her studio, the one depicting a woman engaging in fellatio. Like me, nobody else would feel arousal from gazing at that image. If somebody were to grow aroused at the image, it could only occur if that person happened to have a very passionate nature or if the painting were not modern enough. In the painting, I discovered techniques that strived to put distance between the self and the object, so I felt the image was abstract. The fine wrinkles around the woman's mouth and the tiny beads of sweat on her brow left me feeling rather alienated, and the techniques borrowed from cartoons such as the use of primary colors and such comic-book lines as "Oh, Great!" were employed with the aim of establishing reflexive distance from the object.

From Duchamp's readymades to Dada, Assemblage, Pop Art, Hyperrealism, and Fluxus, among others, the whole of modern art can be explained just through kitsch. In the fake paradise lacking order and truth, only play becomes a comfort for us, and humans who desire limitless freedom find more and more freedom through play. Like many modern artists who believe that kitsch is the only possible art in a fake paradise where reality is lost, she too had fallen for the temptation of kitsch. And correspondingly, she believed that in a world where love was not possible, sex was the only alternative.

Feeling a bit miserable, I walked slowly through the city's downtown morning, my heart too impure to return home. For some time already, home had no longer offered hope for me. To find hope, I would need to walk longer through the streets, so I turned my steps toward the city library. It was close to ten, about the time when department stores and banks open to welcome their customers. I walked wearily and finally arrived at the city library. Fumbling in my pocket, I found a one-hundred-won coin and put it into the ticket box to get a ticket for a seat.

Entering the library, I looked for the bathroom first and washed my face one more time before heading to the magazine room, where I sat down on a chair. Every day, new papers and new journals were printed and published. Before starting to read the day's newspaper and the journals that I hadn't yet had the chance to look at, I opened the book of Munch's paintings that she'd given me. As if to steal a glance at my embarrassed heart, I somewhat nervously turned to the page where the painting

Puberty was printed. Yet, the picture was not there. Although the book was clearly the same as the one I had always looked at in the bookstore for imported books, the picture was not there where it should have been. I checked for the page number and discovered that the page was missing. Either the book had been incorrectly bound, or somebody must have torn the picture out. This took on symbolic meaning for me. I felt my heart ache as if my own puberty had been stolen.

Lost in my musings, I was looking at the empty page when a quiet voice from behind called my name. Looking up, I saw Hyun-jae standing there.

"Eh," I said, surprised, "what happened to you? Didn't you go to school?"

"I stayed overnight somewhere else with some guys," she said. "I came here directly after getting up this morning."

We left the magazine room for a lounge. She told me that she had seen me going out with a woman the previous day when she had come to see me at the club.

"Who was the woman?" Hyun-jae asked. "She looked nice."

"She was an artist," I explained. "I went to her studio with her."

"An artist? What did you do there?"

"Oh, my image was taken. She took it away completely."

"Image? What do you mean?"

I told her about everything that happened that night.

"Really?" Hyun-jae said. "You must have felt good. You must be exhausted."

"No," I admitted, "I feel miserable. You should have called me yesterday when you saw me."

"Well, it wasn't necessary, was it?" Hyun-jae observed. "I also had some fun."

Hyun-jae acted the same as on the day when she had first seen me. She had liked me then and had wanted to sleep with me, but because I hadn't shown any interest, she had gone to a hotel with another guy, as she later told me.

"Who were they this time?" I asked.

"Oh, three university students with money," she said, dismissively. "They had a car, and two other girls and I got in and rode out of town with them. The other two girls they picked up were baby prostitutes."

Sipping cola bought from the vending machine, Hyun-jae, like the fabulous Scheherazade, told me in detail what had happened the previous night.

"The students, hardly deserving of the label, were real trash. Maybe they were the university students who borrowed the English word "betting" to mean competing for sex. They were playboys. The guy who slept with me was rather innocent, at least, but the other two were completely depraved. Utter reprobates. They wanted to do all kinds of things."

"What?"

"They wanted to have group sex," she said. "They've probably done it several times before."

"And?"

"I said no. They seem to have gone ahead with it anyway. I locked the door and had sex with my partner until morning. The silly thing was, he offered me money afterwards and said that he wanted to see me again. He must have thought that I was a prostitute."

She had taken the money.

"I felt strange," she admitted. "If I took the money, I would bc a prostitute, whereas if I refused the money, I would be a lady. Somehow, I preferred to feel like a prostitute. So I took it and tucked it into my bra as he watched."

In the crowded lounge, Hyun-jae carefully slipped her fingers between the buttons on her shirt, so that no one would see. She took the money from her bra, and spread it out in front of me.

"They offered me a lift home," she told me, "but I turned them down and took a taxi because what they were talking about was so childish."

"What was so childish?"

"Oh, the stuff that they were talking about later during breakfast in the hotel room. They were saying that it would be good if there were a demonstration forecast, like a weather forecast, predicting in which streets and places the next demonstration would probably take place. That way, they could avoid those streets and avoid being struck by a Molotov cocktail. I refused their offer to drive me downtown because I grew sick of their talk. I acted the right way, didn't I?"

I smiled foolishly. Hyun-jae's sense of justice sometimes surprised me.

"What should we do with this money?" she wondered.

Hyun-jae and I had each become part-time prostitutes, although I hadn't taken any money.

"It's already too late to go to school, and tomorrow is Sunday," she observed. "Should we take a trip? Should we see the sea? What do you think?"

She begged me to make a trip with her to Busan. I didn't have anything else to do. Newspapers and journals can easily be skipped, and I was tired of the novels that I could finish in five hours. Leaving the library, we went straight to the train station. Although I wanted to check with my mother down in the underground shopping area and tell her that I needed some fresh air for a while, I could not insist on that if Hyun-jae wasn't going to call her family. We left no word and rode south by the ordinary train. With the hearts of prostitutes.

"If we spend time like this," she observed, "we will age very quickly from too many memories."

As our southbound train slowly found the track to Busan among the intricacy of rail lines resembling tangled noodles, I spoke, nearly sighing.

"We either need scrapbooks for all our memories, or a house for organizing the past."

Hyun-jae just looked at me, then turned on her Walkman and, putting her headphones on her ears, said, "Whatever the house, I don't need anyone to live with. A house for the two of us doesn't exist on this earth."

Her words instantly reminded me of a story that I had once read. Printed in an old monthly literary journal, the story was about some young people who decided to make rooms of their own. Four high school students go to an empty house that an uncle of one student has put in their charge, and for the next seventeen days, they imagine themselves making it a place of their own that nobody else can enter or even look into. They say, "The house that we're building won't be a dirty one touched by human hands." The building material wasn't bricks, stones, or cement but something completely new. They imagine that they can build a glass house, "glittering" and "transparent," whose outer shell would shatter and drop away once the house was filled with water and allowed to freeze, precisely the same way a water-filled jar shatters as it freezes.

The title of the story might have been "Glass Castle." They turn a water hose on and, starting with the basement, let the rooms fill and freeze one after another all the way to the third-floor rooms at the top. During the 17th night, while sleeping in a tent on the roof, they hear the sound *tshung*—the sound of something cracking open. But the building doesn't collapse or tilt. When they go down to look, it stands as upright as ever before their eyes, revealing only cracks in its icy walls like shining wounds pouring forth blood, and it towers over them like a huge monster. Like the main character of Lee Sang's "The Wings," crying out, "Let me fly, let me fly, let me fly just one time," the story ends with them shouting, "Break! Break, you dirty walls!"

Consciousness of "interior" and "exterior" selves is first experienced by young people at puberty. At that time, a young person grows vaguely conscious of his self and thus walls himself off from the everyday world. To secure his freedom, he chooses solitude. One character in "Glass Castle" said, "Only when I'm alone does the world belong to me. For me to own the world, all others must die. Only in solitude can one imagine everything." That one can imagine everything only in solitude offers an answer to the question of how to obtain limitless freedom. Limitless freedom is gained by excluding everyone other than oneself and making a wall against the world.

On our train was a group of people setting off for a camping trip. Some played poker while others kept time with their hands and feet to the loud music of Madonna, whose cassette they were playing. What is the psychology of a woman who exhibits her body like a moron? I feel sick whenever I see a woman trying to show off her body like that. Those days, however, everybody, whether man or woman, was in love with Madonna. Several hundred million people on earth had lost their souls to this low-grade moron who showed her bellybutton, wore her underwear on stage, and gyrated while dangling a cross from her neck.

During the entire train ride, we could not decide what to do upon arriving in Busan. Hyun-jae just listened to her Walkman and I read a novel by Conrad. When we got off at the Busan train station, we wondered which beach to go to, Haeundae or Taejongdae. Coincidentally, each of us had already been to one of the two places. After a discussion, we decided to visit Gwangalli, which had as many luxurious motels and restaurants lined up along the coast as there were boats hauled up on the beach.

"Look at those buildings," I told her. "Don't you want to own a building like that, Hyun-jae?"

Hyun-jae's answer was dry. "I don't need one. I can just rent."

That was our generation. We could just rent anything. A house, a room, a car, a video—we could rent it all. If we knew who would rent it out, under what conditions, according to what procedures, for what price, we could rent anything. It was the same with love or sex. The important thing was the information. If we had access to high-quality information, we could rent the world, or so we believed.

Other than stepping out for fresh air along the beach, Hyun-jae and I spent the whole of Saturday and Sunday in our motel room. On Sunday evening, in order not to miss the last train for Daegu, I told Hyun-jae that we needed to leave for the station and get on the train, so that she could attend school on Monday.

"Let's go before it gets too late. If we take a taxi now, we can catch the last train."

Despite my urgings, Hyun-jae didn't move. She lay naked on the bed, a cigarette in her mouth.

"Get up quickly and put on your clothes," I warned. "Otherwise, I'll have to force you!"

Hyun-jae stared at my upset face and said, "Do you want to see how much I hate school? Watch."

She raised her right hand to her face, then moved it slowly toward her breast. Between her thumb and index finger was the burning cigarette.

"Oh, no!" I cried when I understood what she was about to do.

But there was no time to stop her as she extinguished the cigarette by rubbing it into her right breast. She didn't even grimace. Yellowish smoke from her burning flesh spiraled into the air. I rushed to her and grabbed the cigarette from her hand.

"Do you want to die?"

I hurried to the bathroom and wet a towel with cold water. Then I put it on the dime-sized burn, which was inflamed and oozing. Only then did Hyun-jae start to sob.

"Starting tomorrow," she explained, "we have the practice test for the university exam. I don't want to go to school!"

"Okay, we won't go. We'll just do what we want. The test doesn't matter."

I calmed her down, then ran to the drugstore to buy gauze and some burn cream. After her wound was treated with the cream, Hyun-jae smiled with pleasure at being babied. "Hold me, please," she said.

We fooled around for so long that the bedsprings nearly came loose. She said, "My erogenous zones are the real practice test for the university exam. Whenever a practice test approaches, I feel horny."

She told me that she believed in reincarnation and that she was very fearful of being reborn as a high-school student in Korea. "Being reborn as an insect because of my many sins would be much better," she observed.

Moving from the motel to a cheaper hotel, we stayed in Busan until we'd spent all our money. Hyun-jae disliked sunlight and wasted all day lying in the room, listening to the radio or doodling on paper, but at sunset, she went out to the beach and spent hours building sandcastles. Then at night, as I embraced her passionately, she cried out so loudly that the sound echoed throughout the whole hotel.

After a five-day holiday in Busan, I returned home. My mother prepared dinner for me without saying a word. As I was drinking water after finishing the meal, my mother said, "If studying is too hard, you should rest a bit."

Although I almost told her the truth, that I hadn't been attending cram school for a long time, I controlled myself, suppressing the urge. If she heard the truth, she would faint. When I went up to my attic room, there was a packet in front of the door. It was clearly addressed to me, but there was no return address. From the outside, it looked like a book, and when I opened it, I found a poetry journal. On a hunch, I glanced at the table of contents. In one corner, printed vertically, were small letters that caught my eye. They read, "Recommendation of new poet: Go Eun-sun."

With few exceptions, the recommended poems were the ones that I had read in the tearoom some months earlier. In the judging committee's commentary, the praise "internal bleeding of the imagination—poems of a new generation" was printed in bold print, and from some established writers, nonsense such as "imagination of the *fin de siècle*," was written. In the section presenting the winner's views, her image reminded me of the fresh expression of a swimmer: a brightly smiling face still dripping with water immediately after reaching the finish line first. The photo was probably taken when Eun-sun had run to a photo shop immediately after receiving the news of her success.

In the winner's views, such expressions as "suffering," "pain of creation," and "self-flagellating," more appropriate for a masochist, stuck out awkwardly from long, somewhat restless sentences. Rather indifferently but carefully, I read Eun-sun's poems, the comments of the judging committee, and the winner's views. Her poems would probably be accepted as fresh, at least until she had published enough to make a volume. And then? She would probably have more use for those expressions like "suffering," "pain of creation," and "self-flagellating" used in her winner's views.

Lying in the room, I felt anguished, wondering if I should call to congratulate her. Then realizing that a lot of people would already be congratulating her, my anguish seemed rather worthless. That night, too, my sleep was colorless. I dreamt of nothing and heard no sound.

Only the cries of a secondhand book dealer finally awakened me at noon. Hearing his cries, the thought struck me that I should take my brother's books, which were stacked up in a corner of my attic room, and sell them. These books, which my brother had sent me from Seoul, sat poised in the corner of my room, seeming to keep watch over me. An inconvenience, they preyed on my mind like tumor cells in the brain. I opened the little window of my attic room and called the dealer, then carried all my brother's books down to the yard.

For the whole stack, which filled two big noodle boxes, I received only 5000 won. For a mere 5000, I sold off my brother's history books about revolutions in China, Cuba, Vietnam, Nicaragua, and Russia, including the *The History of the Russian Revolution*, and my brother's biographies of revolutionaries like Mao, Gramsci, Rosa Luxemburg, and Franz Fanon, starting with *A Biography of Marx*. Along with all these, I also disposed of my brother's cynicism, comments he had scribbled in red ink, inscribed on the books' margins. My brother wrote on the last page or the title leaf lines in the form of a book review:

> —Lenin was a fighter. Lenin was never defeated. Whenever he fought, he won, won, and won. Nobody could defeat him. Even proletarians couldn't beat him, and at the end, Lenin won out even over the proletarians.
> —The liberation-theory people don't reflect on themselves. They believe that even their own personal faults and selfishness, which spring from within, are caused by external reality and the social structure. Why don't they put their hands on their chests and reflect on themselves?
> —Humans cannot escape from their will to power. If knowledge is considered a form of power, an intellectual is someone who fiercely pursues this will to power.
> —The Communist Party should be one of many parties for proletarians. How could only the Communist Party, a mere party, hold power forever?

—We need not criticize Kim Il-sung's hereditary monarchy. It's already sufficiently astounding that a Communist country, in which the Communist Party is supposed to safeguard the revolution by ruling only for the proletariat, should ever adopt hereditary succession. How ridiculous it is!

While the secondhand dealer was measuring the weight of "secondhand goods" on the scale, a postcard fell from between the pages of a book. I picked it up and read it. As if to confirm that the sender was a woman, the handwriting was very tidy and round.

—You are a cowardly intellectual who became a Neo-Marxist even before becoming a Marxist. I will *not* see you again! You and your huge brain should disappear from the face of the earth! Jung-min.

My brother's brain might have been a monster not designed for living with people in this country. He always wanted to challenge his abilities. From his hometown to Seoul, from Seoul to New York, in the end, he just might fly from the face of the earth to challenge some aliens to an intellectual duel.

Helping the dealer to load the goods in the pushcart, I saw an English book protruding from among the other stuff. Curious, I pulled it out. *The Empty House*. It was a mystery by Michael Gilbert. I liked the title. I asked the dealer how much it cost.

"Eh," he grunted, "that is a valuable book."

I bought it for 2000 won. The title, *The Empty House*, caught my attention for a moment before giving me the sense that I had found a lost poem. I would be able to read this book, I mused, and maybe become a literary translator. "Literary translator"—it was a spontaneous idea, but it sounded fine to me. So to test my

English, which I'd learned in high school, I decided to translate the book.

I bought a big college notebook and, pressing with nearly enough force to engrave the words onto the paper, wrote on the first page in blue ink the words "*Bin Jip*," Korean for "Empty House." Deciding on this Korean title had taken the whole day. "*Bin Jip*" had been forced to compete with other justifiable titles, such as the Korean for "Lonely House" and "Void House," and also had to fight in an unexpected ambush against "Secret House." After writing the title, I printed under it the author's name, "Michael Gilbert," in smaller letters. Because I could not see any detailed information about the author, I transcribed it in Korean as "Michael" with the "k" sound of the hard English "ch," but if he should turn out to be French, I would need to have transcribed it differently in Korean, as "Michael" with the "sh" sound of the soft English "ch." I then wrote in parentheses: "Harper & Row, 1978."

Quoted on the novel's opening page was a single stanza from a Yeats poem whose final line implied that Gilbert had borrowed his title from it, or maybe that he had been inspired by that poem. I started translating the poem first.

I found that stanza alone insufficient for me to understand Yeats' words, so I went to the library and borrowed a collection of Yeats' poems. Then, I better understood the meaning of the stanza that I had just translated. The poem was about modern people, caught in the crumbling house of civilization, appealing to the bees, symbols of creativity, to return home once again.

With a lunch box and an English-Korean dictionary, I went to the library every day, just as I used to. I thought the novel was clear and easy to read, but translating it was not such an easy task. I struggled with *The Empty House* all through June and July. Despite my working on it for over a month, less than one fifth had been translated. During this time, Hyun-jae never showed up, not even once. I assumed that she must have gotten into trouble at school for skipping the practice test for the university entrance exam. At any rate, her absence didn't affect my daily schedule at all.

One day in August, I encountered Eun-sun at a literary lecture that took place in the YMCA. She was sitting in a seat several rows ahead of me next to her boyfriend, who was wearing a military shirt with the sleeves rolled up. The lecturer was a literary critic whom I liked, but my fierce jealousy over Eun-sun left me feeling uncomfortable, so I could not concentrate on his lecture.

"We are now, near the end of the 20th century, facing a new century, the 21st. Modern society, with its enormous degree of acceleration, is changing so fast that even all of the knowledge and technology accumulated in the last 2000 years could never predict the next ten years. It is my job in today's lecture to forecast how art will change and respond to a 'modernity' that transforms what mankind has accomplished in the previous 2000 years every 24 hours."

Pushing thick, plastic glasses up the bridge of his nose, the young critic in his twenties stared at his audience. There were seats unoccupied, and the audience numbered only about twenty people, including the organizers, journalists, and literature specialists, leaving only a few members of the general public.

"Technological development and formidable machinery might threaten to hand art from professionals over to non-professionals. Artists facing such a threat will try to secure their position with some strategy for making *themselves* non-professional in order to nullify the threat itself. An entire host of threats has the potential to ruthlessly trample underfoot the mystique of creativity that persuades us that art can be created only by a few special people and that true art is only possible in the hands of geniuses. First . . ."

Looking to the front, I saw Eun-sun appear to write down the number "1" in an open notebook. Her boyfriend in the next seat innocently watched Eun-sun taking notes.

". . . through the development of computer technology, even those without creativity will be able to write novels and make music. Hyperfiction, made by computer manipulation, is already on display in its great variety, and according to a Western specialist in pop music, the 1990s will be a time when even those without an ability to write music will compose and enjoy it through computers. In fact, music made that way is already being listed on popular music charts in the West. We are living in a time where we hand over creativity, a genuine ability of humans, to computers. Maybe that is why poets and writers often discuss computers as the main topic in their meetings."

Eun-sun, listening to the lecture, was nodding along with other people whom I didn't know. They didn't seem to be students. Then, I realized that Eun-sun didn't belong to the few members of the general public who had come to this YMCA lecture. She was now the poet that she wished to be.

"Second, in the case of literature, through the development of publishing and print technology, anybody can now easily publish a book. Earlier, publishing a book of poetry was such a harrowing and difficult task, almost like selling a house, but these days, it is so easy and cheap that the opportunity is open to many non-professionals to publish a poetry book. Of course, cunning commercialism and the unprofessionalism of newspapers and the broadcast media played a role, so that by the end of the 1980s, for example, countless poetry books had been published by such amateurs as singers, homemakers, and high school students, and even poetry books of collected scribblings by anonymous individuals. Personally, I trust the procedures of the literary establishment, but the monster of 'modernity' tries to reduce initiation rites as much as possible, or even get rid of these entirely. The speed of an accelerating process that omits the initiation rites in every area of culture surely results from the logic of capitalism, with its tendency to promote mass production and consumption and which gives rise to our throwaway culture."

But isn't it also the logic of capitalism to produce more complicated stages? Through continuous subdividing and classifying, capital is able to produce more products and more consumption. Capital simplifies the process of production and distribution or multiplies their stages, depending on its pursuit of maximum profits.

"Third, the non-professionals' demand for abolishing distinctions and their disregard for specialists motivates professional artists to react by turning themselves into non-specialists, which amounts to accepting the demand to abolish distinctions. We could say that the transition from modernism to postmodernism means a transition from professionals to non-professionals. Whereas modernism needed the category of an individual self, or an independent space, the postmodern self declares an end to the *self*-centered psychological condition, together with the end of the self or individual. Whereas modernist writers imbued themselves with such authoritative godly attributes as purity, rarity, and the aura, postmodernist writers have come down to the public through self-openness, through the processes of borrowing, quoting, extracting, or adapting."

It had become the fashion to attach the prefix "post" to every situation. Unfortunately, the relationship between Eun-sun and me had already long entered the "post" stage, even though making a clear distinction between the two periods was not easy, much as with other movements where the prefix "post" is used.

"Rosenberg said that in a technological era, artists would remain the last non-specialists, and in fact, in our post-industrial society, which daily promotes specialization and a division of labor, the arts might tend, by contrast, to become an area for non-specialists. In my opinion, however, this phenomenon of robbing the specialists of their specialty is not limited only to the arts but occurs in every area of life simultaneously. For example, the oversupply of personal computers encourages people nowadays to become specialists in everything, beckoning from various places, saying, 'You can become an expert in this field.' Conversely, such an invitation and beckoning robs specialists of their specialty, and this process of invitation, beckoning, and robbing forces itself upon us due to the speed of 'modernity' and its rapid acceleration. For this reason, even tiny little elementary school kids are eager to learn how to use the computer so as not to fall behind. That's the reality today."

I had been staring at the back of Eun-sun's head. There, like one face of Janus, appeared the face of the other woman, the cosmopolitan artist who traveled between Munich and New York. Although she had taken away my image, I silently thanked her for explaining the speeding, accelerated world to me.

"I would say that the crisis of the self is the crisis of the specialist. The recent issue of collective creation illuminates the crisis of the self and the specialist from a different perspective than the threats that I've just listed. Collective creation, which has evolved from co-creation to cooperatively organized creation, has such characteristics as non-specialism, speed, and anonymity, all of which threaten self-ness and professionalism, rather severely limiting the artist's capability and art's self-control. We could say that the theory of collective creation, which organizes its expression against pressures managed systematically, is based upon the premise that it already controls the artist's capability and art's self-control to some degree."

The lecture went on for about forty minutes, and after it ended, around twenty minutes remained for questions and answers. Eun-sun's boyfriend stood up and spent some time trying to defend the collective creation that the lecturer had criticized. He even claimed that it alone could become real literature.

"Group literature resulted from the people's demand to build a people's literature and is designed to present an effective fight against fascism and American imperialism. Without first considering the background to group literature's formation, to put it on the same level as the Yankee's computer literature and to talk about the self-crisis or the destruction of art's self-control, is, I think, the shortsightedness of an intellectual literary critic with an intention of misleading others about the essence of group literature. In the grand scheme of things, what meaning does the end of modernism have for our nation? Also, how will postmodernism solve the many contradictions of our divided nation?"

I could not understand the psychology of a university student who wore a military uniform as casual wear, especially someone involved in the student movement. Time passed, and as the questions and answers grew less interesting, Eun-sun and her boyfriend got up from their seats. At that point, Eun-sun saw me sitting behind her.

"It's been a long time since I last saw you," I said. "Congratulations!"

"Yeah," she replied. "Won't you come out with us, Adam?"

"Okay," I agreed, "let's go somewhere."

We headed for the alley where all the drinking places frequented by university students were located, found one without many customers, and settled in at a table. I quickly got myself drunk and started behaving in a rather intolerable manner. I could not stand Eun-sun's boyfriend at all.

"Hey mister," I taunted, "I guess you go to demonstrations in that military uniform. You must look really great throwing Molotov cocktails."

He just smiled. Even that smile, I didn't like. Although I had decided not to feel inferior to university students, maintaining my resolve was not easy in the presence of Eun-sun's boyfriend.

"You look like you're trying to seduce a woman, wearing that thing."

In the precise moment that I finished my sentence, his fist flew at me. I was struck by the direct, full force and immediately crashed to the floor, my nose already starting to bleed.

"This guy is a real asshole, isn't he?" her boyfriend said.

Eun-sun tossed me a white handkerchief and followed her boyfriend out, calling behind her, "Adam, you just can't stop barking, like a dog!"

The handkerchief was quickly soaked red with blood. I was surprised. Was there so much Communism in my body? The Red and the red blood kept gushing out. Are people born possessed of Communism from birth? The white handkerchief that Eun-sun had tossed grew thoroughly red, like a flag of the enemy. The enemy's flag, drenched with my blood, looked so red and beautiful.

It is said that female pirates who founded a community in the West Indies in the 1760s first used a red flag. They called it *joli rouge*, meaning red and beautiful. After that, it was used for signaling an attack by English seamen and sailors agitating for strikes. Having over time taken on an ever clearer meaning of protest and the fight for freedom, it came to symbolize the Communist movement.

Meanwhile, it was close to mid-August, and I was putting all my energy into translating *The Empty House*. "Right," I thought, "it will become a work translated with all my energy."

The Olympic Games were fewer than 40 days away. Newspapers and broadcasters were busy every day with stories about the Olympics, but people in my neighborhood were prohibited from peddling on the streets. That was the reality behind the slogan "hand in hand." Nobody talked about who would profit or who would lose. It made me want to go off backpacking in a deep forest when the Olympic Games started.

One mid-August afternoon, as I was sitting in the library translating *The Empty House*, Hyun-jae came to see me. About two months had passed since we had last seen each other. She didn't have stockings on, maybe because of the heat, and was wearing a short skirt, as always. She looked the same as she had two months earlier, except she was a bit thinner and no longer had a Walkman bound to her waist; instead, she held in her hand a cassette player the size of a lunchbox.

"Let's get out of here quickly," she urged. "We should have a memorial ceremony."

Without knowing what was going on, I went out with her, taking all of my stuff with me. "What kind memorial ceremony?" I asked. "For whom?"

"Roy Buchanan is dead," she told me. "Apparently, he killed himself."

Hyun-jae answered so naturally, as if a man from her neighborhood had died.

"How did you find out?"

"You know I have my headphones on all the time."

According to her, he was feeling insecure in the days leading up to a concert and had overdosed on some drug.

"Last night," she said, "I was listening to a radio program, and the DJ talked about it. I was very sad."

We went to a music shop to buy a used guitar for 50,000 won, then bought a canister of kerosene elsewhere, and took a bus to Gangjung. She asked me, "Aren't you sad? You also liked Roy Buchanan."

I didn't answer. On the asphalt street leading out of town, a group of motorcyclists was roaring along. Each biker was around twenty years old and belonged to the speed group, for they valued as the only important thing the forward rush at breakneck speed. They were narcissists intoxicated with their own velocity. In a society where speed is a virtue, they compared themselves to flowers.

The speed group is open to the outer world and continuously expands its territory toward new, yet-unconquered land. For them, only new things bring pleasure and only conquering gives life meaning. But someday, they will suddenly realize that their speed and the earth's surface are limited. Whatever speed they attempt, they cannot go beyond the limit of human beings, and the distance their speed can take them is already set by the finite extent of the earth's surface.

The audio group, on the other hand, discovers ever new meanings, even from listening repeatedly to the same melody. They peer into their inner selves and try to create there not an earthly landscape but a heavenly one that cannot be reached by anybody, whereas the speed group is open to the outer world and is always rushing to find new land. The speed group can experience ecstasy only through riding their motorbikes, but the audio group can continue to experience ecstasy even after turning an audio system off. Moreover, whereas the speed group cannot move fast without a motorbike, the audio group can create music even without an audio system. This means that the audio group is much more self-reliant than the speed group. But among the audio group, there are some quasi-audio individuals similar to the speed group, those who are continuously looking for new songs and trying to keep up with fads. They are people trapped by a need for new things, and are alienated from their true selves.

Hyun-jae and I got off in Gangjung, put the guitar on the sand bank, and poured the kerosene all over it. We put a cassette tape of Roy Buchanan's music into the cassette player and began listening to his most famous song, "The Messiah Will Come Again." Hyun-jae, who was about to strike a match over the kerosene-drenched guitar, looked up at me.

"Don't we need a poem for the memorial?" she asked. "Compose a poem spontaneously."

"I can't. It's too sudden."

"You said that you were great in high school. So why not?"

I started to recite a spontaneous poem, or something like a poem, which might be the last one in my life. The sad sound of Buchanan's guitar, the burning guitar raising bluish flames, and the white sand bank all moved me to compose this poem:

Perfect, almost perfect, perfect was
Roy, you yourself the guitar.
Creating renditions, techniques,
Roy, guitarist of guitarists.
Now you are gone,
And only the music now waits for the promised messiah.

Before you died,
I knew that
Life was one,
Death was one,
Fingers were ten,
Guitar strings were six.

But with your death,
We must play the guitar with one string gone,
An imperfect guitar with five strings,
A defective guitar.

After I had finished reciting the poem, and when the last notes of "The Messiah Will Come Again" had died away and the flames burning the guitar had died down, in that order, Hyun-jae, tears in her voice, cried out.

"Why did you say that the guitar is only defective, you fool? Guitar music is dead now."

"No," I disagreed, "the guitar and its music never die, not ever."

In the history of rock music, there have been three cases when someone's death has been remembered with the highest tribute: "The music is dead." Buddy Holly, Elvis, and John Lennon were those three. But what does the eulogy mean for them, and can it serve to comfort even the living?

"The guitar not only won't die," I added, "but it also shouldn't die."

Watching the sky turn red-black over the river, we listened to "Still I'm Sad" by the Yardbirds as the appropriate song to follow Roy's "The Messiah Will Come Again." This music was appropriate to commemorate someone's death because of its similarity to Gregorian Chant, and moreover, the importance of the group playing the song made it the most appropriate for remembering our most beloved guitarist. The Yardbirds were a band formed in the mid-sixties in England that had been led by Eric Clapton, Jeff Beck, and Jimmy Page, who were regarded as the three best rock guitarists, in that order. When that band broke up, Jimmy Page, trying to form a new Yardbirds, found three new members and renamed the band Led Zeppelin, which opened a new page in rock history.

After the fire had subsided completely, Hyun-jae and I hurried back to town.

"Why are you hurrying so much?" I complained. "Let's slow down."

"I have a reason," she said, and explained that she worked in a coffee room for men after school.

"Yesterday, the president of a company wanted to go out with me. He was my father's age and was so shameless. I told him that we could see each other next week. I don't know what to do."

Hyun-jae's behavior surprised me, for she needed to satisfy neither a financial lack nor any curiosity.

"Don't be too surprised," she admonished. "I have many friends at school who work in such drinking places. They all do it because there is no escape for them."

I felt that Hyun-jae was moving in a bad direction. The end of a bad thing is easily imaginable long before it happens, even the worst cases. But I could do nothing to influence her at all. I could not move even a hair. We parted from each other when we arrived downtown again. While leaving, I glimpsed her back, and from behind, she seemed like an urban ghost.

I gave up translating the murder mystery. A leftist media critic in the West maintained, in explaining the social function of the genre, that the mystery quells the righteous hatred that the petit bourgeois class holds against the greater bourgeoisie, replacing it with hatred of the murderer in mystery fiction, and also nullifies the real-life will to revolt. In mysteries, it was always the rich who were killed off, and they were killed off because of their corruption and immorality. So by reading a mystery where the rich are killed one after another, the petit bourgeois class can rid itself of its hatred toward a richer, more powerful class.

Also the mystery emphasizes human helplessness before death, depicting the rich as helpless at the hands of their killers despite having a stately mansion, perfect crime-prevention devices and armed guards, and the enormous power of money. Through this emphasis, the mystery succeeds in replacing the real conflicts faced by the petit bourgeois class with the concept of fate and so avoids real problems.

The critic goes on to argue that the mystery stands over the common people, ensuring we lack the knowledge and wisdom required for solving the mystery, representing our lack of capacity for running social and political institutions. Moreover, the mystery, in its implications, leads us to think that we should put people wiser and more competent than ourselves in charge of running society, which will result in the state being kept as it is, precisely as the bourgeoisie want.

I didn't completely agree with his analysis. For his analysis to make sense, the petit bourgeois class would have to be reading a lot of mystery novels. And not just a lot. More to the point, precisely those people who would give up on the revolution after reading mystery novels would have to become readers of the genre. But it is hard to imagine that the petit bourgeois class, which is provided neither time nor opportunity for education, would become the general readership for mystery novels. The mystery is rather preferred by the wealthier class, which has more opportunity for education and more leisure time. The petit bourgeois class, if it had any time, would select a magazine or grab a comic book.

Of course, the reason that I gave up translating the mystery novel was not because I didn't want to participate in the bourgeois' strategy of manipulating people through the discourse of the mystery. To state the reason openly, my mistake from the beginning had been to think the mystery too easy. In fact, translating that mystery novel required special knowledge in genetics, assessing damage, real estate transactions, geographical facts, and military information, among other things showing up in the book, all of which kept my hand incessantly paging through dictionaries. Moreover, my excessive desire to experience the "pain of creativity" from the translation work posed a problem. I had believed that translating would lead me to more creativity, and I wanted to experience the suffering of productivity. But translating didn't require suffering or result in creativity. It was just tedious labor. I desired to create something. My expectations about enjoying the pleasure of creativity through translating remained unfulfilled. I took *The Empty House* to a secondhand bookshop.

"How much would you pay for this?" I asked.

The owner of the secondhand bookshop merely glanced at the book and said that he wouldn't buy it because no customer would ever buy a novel in a foreign language. He said that I could instead exchange it for a book in his shop. I felt a bit spiteful toward the secondhand goods dealer who had talked about the value of the book and had sold it to me for 2000 won even though no secondhand bookshop would ever buy it. I exchanged *The Empty House* for two dusty pocketbook novels published by Samjungdang.

Before the Olympic Games, at their peak, and on the day after they ended, there occurred three important incidents that also involved me. Only for these reasons will I forever remember the Seoul Olympics.

The first incident was the news that Eun-sun had been arrested for writing a poem titled "Land of Youth." Because I went to the magazine room every morning, I happened to be reading a local evening newspaper the morning after it had been printed, and near the bottom of a page in the news section, I came across a photo of Eun-sun, her forehead jutting toward the camera as if she were frightened of something, along with an abbreviated article about her:

> Go Eun-sun (19), a freshmen university student, is under investigation by the city police because her poem titled "Land of Youth" allegedly encourages and commends North Korea. It is reported that Miss Go published the poem last week in her university newspaper, thereby enhancing North Korea's image. Miss Go was officially acknowledged as a poet in June this year by a poetry journal.

I read and re-read the newspaper article about Eun-sun, looking at her picture many times, then re-read the article several more times, repeatedly looking at the picture. I began to feel rather amused. Eun-sun was hardly, by any means, one to ever embellish the image of North Korea. The youngest daughter of a local, high-ranking government official, a girl full of vanity and selfishness who had memorized Choi Seung-ja's poems just a few months before and who had became an officially recognized poet by imitating those poems? For such a girl to suddenly become a rebel willing to violate the laws of national security would be impossible, unless it were possible to transform a sheep into a wolf. I then recalled something that she had once said to me in one of the hotel rooms that she and I used to rent during the month we spent together.

"Watch," she told me, "Kim Il-sung and Kim Jong-il are on TV."

We were almost out of breath, having turned the TV on immediately after a bout of passionate sex, and there was news about North Korea. On the screen, a crowd of several thousand people were sitting in a place resembling a gymnasium, and the father and son were shown onstage, clapping along with the crowd. The film had been taken during some meeting or other of the people, and whenever news about North Korea was aired on TV in the South, this scene was usually shown.

"I've come to hate Kim Il-sung and dislike North Korea," she explained, "because of the hand clapping."

"What do you mean?" I asked. "You hate Kim Il-sung because of hand clapping?"

"Watch that film," she said. "Don't you get it?"

According to Eun-sun, for a socialist country where everybody was supposed to be equal, the styles of hand clapping differed too much. As I watched the screen again, I saw that she had a point. The great crowd, thousands of people strong, was clapping so quickly that their hands almost couldn't be seen, but the father and son were clapping their hands at a very lazy speed.

"If there is such a difference in hand clapping," Eun-sun emphasized, "how can equality be possible? Also, with the clapping motions in such perfect order, how can there be freedom?

Moreover, they envision a hereditary dynasty, so how can it be a democratic republic of the people?"

"Okay," I said, "I don't know very much about North Korea because I have never been there. But isn't it your problem if you like or dislike half of our nation just because of the way some people clap? And you talk about 'hereditary,' but everyone in the South makes connections through family and relatives. The relationships are all personal. Look at the case of ex-President Chun. While he was in power, how many of his relatives plundered our country? Hereditary dynasty is obvious from the outside, so it becomes a target of attack, but personal connections through family members and relatives are hidden here in the South and result in even worse things."

No matter what I said, she didn't try to understand my argument. Because of the way he clapped, Kim Il-sung was bad. If a person with such views had really written a poem praising North Korea only a few months later, something else must have been going on. Perhaps the unification movement had incited her to write such a poem, including the "Council of Universities' Representatives," which had suggested a meeting of South and North Korean university students prior to the Olympic Games.

September 17th, 1988, was the date of the opening ceremony of the Seoul Olympic Games, and although only two-thirds of the countries participated, the Seoul Games were better than the ones in Moscow or Los Angeles had been. On the morning of the opening ceremony, as I was riding a bus and passing by close to the Daegu Bank's main building, I saw a man playing the tambourine. Dressed in a white shirt, dark blue suit pants, and black shoes, he was playing the tambourine and smiling. The tidily dressed man, perhaps in his early thirties, was drooling through his open mouth, his head twisted to the left, and he was shaking the tambourine with his right hand, pulling it in to his chest, then out again like a yo-yo, hitting it with his left hand.

People on their way to work had gathered around him. He seemed crazy. One of those standing around twirled his index finger in a circle near his own temple. The bus that I was riding passed by the man playing the tambourine, but the image remained in my mind for a long time. Why had he gone crazy? And why was he playing the tambourine at the foot of the bank building? The whole day, I imagined all kinds of things about the man.

Maybe, it had happened like this. On a stormy evening, the man was sitting at a computer screen, working alone late at night in the office. Close to midnight, a lightning bolt struck that empty building, and an electrical pulse of 100 million volts surged into the lightning rod and down the ground wire into the earth, but along the way induced a surge back into the man's computer. Remember, this is just my imagination. Anyway, the high-voltage electricity thus induced pulsed into the man's finger and shocked him severely as he was working at the computer. The man instantly went insane, and the very next day, a clear sunny day, he became the tambourine man who cries his lonely chant within a forest of grey buildings.

After that, the tambourine man would show up unexpectedly in my imagination, again and again, bothering me. I would hear the sound of the tambourine, and with closed eyes see the tambourine man clearly in my mind. Smiling shyly and shaking the tambourine, he talked to me. "You will become a tambourine man! You will become an elite like me after graduate school! After earning good grades and studying for tests, you will work in a building worth 50 trillion won. You will also work on a computer until late at night, like me! And then, the day after a stormy, late night working, you will become a tambourine man who smiles alone in the forest of grey buildings! Those who worked at computers till late in the night during an evening of thunder and wind-driven rain will all become tambourine men! They will become the crazy ones who smile alone on sunny streets!"

At the end of September, when the Olympic Games were reaching their peak, a second incident happened that would make it impossible for me to ever forget the Seoul Olympics for the rest of my life. It also brought me the turntable that I had wished for. Until then, I would go every day to a small audio shop, about 12–15 square meters in size, located on a corner downtown and look into the shop window. The shop was small but so famous for offering only the best audio systems that it had been showcased in a music magazine. On that unforgettable day, rain was falling, and when I looked into the shop, the clerk who usually worked there was absent, and a middle-aged man who seemed to be the owner was sitting on the sofa. I began slowly scrutinizing the new Marantz model, which had been on display since the previous day. At that moment, the door opened and the middle-aged man tending the shop called me over.

"Hey you," he said, "it's raining. You can come in and look."

His low, soft voice surprised me. It was well-matched with the rain that had been drizzling since morning.

"No," I replied, "I'm not going to buy anything."

"That doesn't matter," he told me. "I know that you come here every day. I want to talk to you."

A bit embarrassed, I went in. In fact, I had no umbrella, but I entered the shop not because I wished to escape being rained on but because I possessed a powerful desire to see the audio systems displayed inside.

"Do you want anything?" the man asked. "I can sell you something at cost."

"No, I'm really just looking."

I saw, in the shop's display case, amps made by Audio Research, Mark Levinson, and Quad, all of which I had heard about but had glimpsed only in magazines.

"You must be very interested in audio systems," the man observed.

"I'm interested only in turntables," I replied.

"A turntable? That's a technical term not used by many people. 'Turntable' sounds somewhat odd, don't you think? Most people call them record players. Alright, is there any one you like specifically?"

"Actually," I admitted, "I don't know much about the products."

"For a record player, Garrard and Thorens are okay. Linn is also quite good. Would you like a cup of coffee?"

"No, thanks," I said, declining the offer. "I'm fine. I should go."

"Wait. You're my customer." He plugged the coffee pot in. "You're a music lover, not the kind of person who hangs around in an audio shop."

"A music lover?"

"Usually," he explained, "the people who listen to music through playback equipment are divided in two groups: Music Lovers and Electronic Listeners. The former love music and don't argue about whether some part of a tone is good or bad. Whenever they play a record or tape, they listen intently to the music, trying to get as close as possible to the live performance. By contrast, the latter are more interested in the technology and invest a lot of money in continually changing it. Their interest in the technology has no limit, and they tirelessly challenge the finest technical equipment. They only focus on the precision of the tone and forget about the music, the most important thing."

While he was talking, the water began to boil. Outside, the drizzling rain continued to drench the streets, and in my head, I was connecting the Music Lover to the audio group and the Electronic Listener to the speed group. He continued talking.

"As for the Lovers, they are less interested in the characteristics of the technology, such as talking about 'the resolving power' or the need for 'very broad frequency bandwidth.' They wouldn't complain much if tones are not too limited but have some degree of breadth. Listeners, on the other hand, never listen to music for a long period of time. They listen only for brief periods and obtain pleasure from hearing the clear, sharp, distinctive tones felt through the measured numbers and data rather than the joy of the music itself. They also don't listen to the music as a whole but as distinguished parts like high tone, low tone, degree of separation, or spontaneity."

He took out cups for coffee and tapped dried coffee into them. His fingers were white and plump.

"The Listeners therefore constantly need new information about the audio systems, and there are lively exchanges among the people in groups organized for this same hobby. Listeners are quite active in organizing such groups of people with this interest in common. Compared to them, the Lovers are relatively passive about the technology and seldom organize groups."

Electronic Listeners, I saw clearly, were like the speed group, always taking off for new lands to conquer. And "Music Lovers" was another name for the audio group, made up of those seeking their own inner worlds, who indulged themselves in creative solitude. I watched as the man poured boiling water into the two cups and added one sugar cube in each.

"As for us sellers," he continued, "we prefer the technology lovers to music lovers. It's better for business. Technology lovers continuously exchange their audio systems for higher quality machines or for new models whenever they think that the sound quality will be better. That process creates profits for us. And the audio companies continually bring new products onto the market, responding to the Electronic Listeners' whims. They embrace each other, so to speak. Thus far in the history of the audio business, almost no company stingy about producing new products has survived."

We drank our coffee. As if he had suddenly remembered, he

put a record on the turntable. Some crossover genre of guitar music was playing.

"McIntosh," he remarked.

For the first time in my life, I listened to a record played on a McIntosh. The sound was delicate and expansive, and the fusion jazz of Bob James and Earl Klugh fit well with the drizzling rain.

"What audio system do you have at home?" he asked. "I can select one to fit it."

"Well, actually," I admitted, "I don't own an audio system. I have a mid-sized cassette player, a very old model, and I want to have it connected to a turntable for listening to records."

He set his cup on the table and smiled. It was a strained smile, as if he was trying not to hurt my feelings.

"Hey," he told me, "there are many ways to get what you want. Of course, everything has its price."

He then offered to give me a record player if I would stay overnight with him, and I thought that this was not such a bad suggestion. Not because of the turntable, but because his suggestion was such a ridiculous one. Of course, his suggestion would not have been worth the humiliation of self-prostitution, certainly not that of losing one's purity, or even having one's cherry popped. But I assumed that it would be nothing special, more like just taking a crap. So I accepted his suggestion and watched him sitting, intoxicated in his own fantasy for a moment.

"Should we go somewhere first to cheer up a bit?" he asked.

"Where?"

"Some place like a gay club," he suggested. "If you don't like that idea, we could go to a nice restaurant or hotel bar."

"Let's do the sex right away," I said.

He looked at me and smiled softly, the smile of one revealing himself as a gay lover. "Then let's go to my place."

He closed his shop and drove me to his mansion in the

suburbs. In his car, with the cool wind blowing gently from the vents of the air conditioner set on low, he said, "I feel something spiritual with a man's body. The thighs without fat, the hard hips, and the smooth breast without sag are different from a woman's fat body."

His bedroom was quite big, and the bed was extremely large. He pointed to the bathroom and told me that I should take a shower first, explaining, "The first step toward becoming a homosexual is concern that the other feels clean."

When I returned from washing, clothed again, I found a bottle of whisky and a platter full of fruits arranged on the big bed. As I was drinking whisky and eating fruit, he came out of the bathroom after his own shower. After drying himself, he wrapped the towel around his waist, sat down on the bed, and also began drinking whisky and chewing on some fruit. Finally, we both took everything off. Naked, he bent under the bed, pulling out a cot that was not yet assembled.

"Just watch," he said. "I will put it together quickly."

"Do you need another bed?"

"It's complicated," he told me. "Although being gay is usually simple, it's a complicated thing for me. Take the bed, for example. I can't get an erection unless I'm on the cot. I can sleep with you in a soft, cushiony bed, but I can only penetrate you on this hard cot. So, this is a little bit of equipment for the initial insertion. It's complicated."

Next to such a luxurious bed, the wretched cot didn't look right. After getting the cot put together, he approached me and sat down by my side, acting very affectionate. But it made me feel sick. I could accept lending my hips, if necessary, but kissing a man and tasting his saliva, or being stroked by sticky male hands posed difficult problems that I hadn't thought of.

"Hey," he said, "foreplay is indispensable to making love with someone of the same sex, but the foreplay in our case is not with our bodies. How easy lovemaking would be if it were possible with the body only. But making love with someone of the same sex is not possible with the body alone. As I told you before, the important thing is the soul, a consensus of souls. That's important. You're closing the gate to that now. Open your soul."

Tossing and turning the whole night, we tried to connect his soul to my body, but that didn't go very well. When my body became hot, his soul became cool, and when his soul became somewhat warm again, my body began to close down. Lovemaking with someone of the same sex seemed to be either purely platonic or merely biological. Aside from the disconnection with him, my own body and soul wouldn't even connect with each other.

By the early morning, he could delay no longer, so he let me lie on my belly in the cot.

"Without a consensus of souls," he said, "it's no better than masturbation."

He put some lube between my buttocks and inserted his sleek penis. I shuddered because it felt as if a pair of tweezers were probing an open wound.

Dismounting from my body after a quick ejaculation, he told me, "The shape of our souls didn't fit. Next time, we can try to make it work. It might work next time." He then went to the large bed and fell into a deep sleep. I didn't move to his bed but slept in the cot.

That night, I dreamed a lot, and most of my dreams had something to do with toilets. For example, although I tried hard to pull the chain for the water, the toilet wouldn't flush, or the string wouldn't even pull. Rising from the toilet, raw sewage was creeping up above my ankles. Suddenly, the toilet door opened, and a cleaning lady in blue uniform and hygienic cap poured water into the toilet. Ah, my mother . . .

The next morning, just as promised, the man gave me a turntable. "This is a Japanese Technics, costs about 800,000 won.

On top of that, a cartridge worth 400,000 won has been built in."

It was a turntable connected to a Fisher tube amp and was set up in his mansion's living room.

"I could give you all this," he offered.

"Don't even say such a silly thing," I said. "I don't think that my anus was worth that much."

He offered to drive me home. Although I didn't like that idea very much, I accepted because of the turntable. I settled into the front seat after first sliding the turntable onto the rear seat, because having it on my knee like a war trophy seemed ridiculous. He said nothing as he drove. The morning rush hour streets were crowded with people and cars. At one point, we stopped before a crosswalk when the traffic light changed to red. There must have been a school nearby because a crowd of elementary school children crossed in front of our car. He watched the children greedily. I felt disgusted.

"I'll get out and walk," I told him.

I got out and took the turntable from the rear seat. I can understand an adult satisfying his sexual desires with another adult, but I cannot accept a pedophile. That sort of sex takes a child, defenseless in mind and body, and turns that child into an object of sexual desire. A public, organized pedophile group in America maintains that children are oppressed into being denied their right to experience sex and are alienated from their own sexuality. Their slogan supposedly says, "Sex before eight, or else it's too late."

After I closed the door and was standing in the street, he spoke to me from the rolled down window. "You might need an amp. Come by if you want."

What a crazy bloke. He thought that I had slept with him for the turntable and believed that I would sleep with him again to get the amp. Extolling his theory on the consensus of souls in bed, he might have seduced a lot of young boys.

When I got home, I connected the turntable to my cassette radio, but they looked so foreign next to each other—like "the chance meeting on a dissecting table of a sewing-machine and an umbrella" in Lautréamont's prose-poem "Maldoror." An old cassette radio connected to a turntable worth 800,000 won! At least I had obtained a turntable, but I now faced another problem. I didn't have a single record. I looked for one at my leisure, stopping by a secondhand shop near the Blue Bridge several times. There one could buy bootleg copies or legitimate recordings. I bought a few rare albums there. In particular, a bootleg copy of a live concert by Vanilla Fudge and a double-album legitimate recording of Steely Dan were very special, and an original record of the female singer Charo, whom I had never heard of before, brought me as much joy as picking up a precious stone from the mud that nobody cared about.

But there were limits to seeking records in a secondhand shop. Most of them were useless, and some records by bands worth listening to were seriously damaged and were distorted or scratchy when played. Perhaps expert collectors might buy records regardless of damage or noise. Who knows, they might even enjoy the noises on damaged records.

After getting the turntable, I adjusted my daily schedule a bit. From morning to noontime, in my attic bedroom, I listened to the records as I read pocketbooks that I had bought in a secondhand bookshop for 300 won each. Because my mother left the house early in the morning, she did not suspect me. The sound quality coming through the old, used cassette radio was not very good, but it was still sweeter than any music from an upscale lounge.

After lunch, I left for the library, where I continued the same lifestyle as before. If there was any change, it was that instead of standing before an audio shop's display window, I was now standing before a record shop window staring at new album jackets.

Looking at album covers was more interesting than gazing at the quality of some pictures on display in an art exhibition. Korean record jackets offered nothing special, but the record jackets of imported records were often beautiful and artistic.

One day, I saw Hyun-jae selecting a cassette from a record shop in the central downtown area. She was wearing a short skirt as always—as if it were her uniform—and a sleeveless running shirt. I watched her through the shop window. Seen through the window, she looked no different from a normal teenage girl. But in reality, how much she was suffering! Hyun-jae quickly chose any cassette and came out.

"Hi," I greeted. "It's been a long time since I last saw you."

"Oh, what are you doing here?" she asked. Terribly short-sighted, she pushed her plastic glasses, which were round like bicycle wheels, up onto her nose, and she seemed happy to see me.

"What did you buy?" I asked.

"A tape by Jim Morrison," she said. "I'd listened to his old tape so much that the tape got tangled, and I couldn't play it any more. By the way, what's that you're holding under your arm?"

Before reaching the library, I had dropped by the shop near the Blue Bridge, only a half-hour's walk away. I usually didn't listen to progressive rock because I didn't like its ostentatious pedantry, but I had paid 50 cents for a legitimate recording, "Pictures at an Exhibition," a piano solo by Mussorgsky but arranged by Emerson, Lake and Palmer.

"It's a record," I replied.

"A record? You told me that you don't own a record player, didn't you?"

"That's right," I confirmed, "I didn't own one, but I'm now able to listen to records."

Offering congratulations, Hyun-jae paid almost 7000 won for a double jacket of Led Zeppelin, a live-concert recording, and gave it to me.

"Thank you," I told her. "I've wanted to have this one for a long time."

"In that case," she said, putting her arm under mine, "we should have a listening session together."

That's how she came to visit my attic room, but once she saw my audio system, she burst out laughing so hard that she had to gasp for breath several times, as if she was close to dying. To be frank, in the bus with her on the way home, I was worried that she might be so shocked upon seeing my audio system that she would faint. So, I was at least fortunate that this didn't happen.

"Don't laugh," I admonished. "All together, it's an audio system worth 1,200,000 won. If I sold this in a secondhand shop, I could buy several cheap Korean record players."

I took the wrapping off the Led Zeppelin jacket, put the first record on the turntable, and we heard Robert Plant introduce the group, saying, "John Henry Bonham, 'Moby Dick'!" An overture, some bars from the lead guitar, the base guitar following, and then John Bonham's solo drumming began. At this point, Hyun-jae lightly removed her shirt.

"What are you doing?" I asked. "Did laughing so much make you crazy?"

She took off her bra and put it under the other clothes she'd already removed. Despite the coin-shaped burn wound, her breasts with their slightly upturned nipples were still cute. Hyun-jae turned up the volume a little more.

"It's said that one should either wear very thin clothes or take them off completely when listening to music. That way, people say, one can live longer. Also, the volume should be as high as possible."

"What's the reason?" I asked.

"Your body gets a massage from the vibrations of the sound waves, which helps the blood circulate. That's why orchestral musicians live longer. I heard that once on the radio. If you wish to live for a long time, you should take off your clothes."

I took off all the clothing on my upper body.

"How did you get it?" she asked.

"Get what?"

"The turntable."

Although it was troubling to relive the experience, I told her how I had gotten the turntable, then added, "So, I gave this turntable a name, Lana. L-A-N-A. Lana."

"How was the sex?" she asked.

"It was like holding my mouth open for a dentist," I said. "It made me shudder. I felt very uncomfortable and wanted it to end quickly."

As we were talking, "Moby Dick," which had become a legendary piece in the history of rock music, was playing. John Bonham's marvelous drum solo filled my attic room through the strange playback equipment, a turntable worth over a million won connected to a cassette radio worth less than 80,000 won. When I had finished talking, Hyun-jae said nothing for a long time. I expected her to make a joke, saying "O my Lord! Forgive this sinful child," but she just lay on her belly in silence, against my expectations, and my heart grew heavy.

"Moby Dick" finished playing. John Bonham had died young from drugs and alcohol four years after performing that piece. Like Jim Morrison, Janis Joplin, and Jimmy Hendrix, the initial of his name was J. When "Whole Lotta Love" followed, Hyun-jae was still lying on her belly in the same spot, maintaining her silence. Except that she now pulled her mini skirt up.

"Do the same thing to me that you experienced," she said.

"No."

"Why not?" she demanded. "Do it quickly. I bought you a record." Still prone, she pulled her underwear down, adding, "In my bag, you'll find some lotion."

I had no desire to do it. In the guise of being free and open with her, I might have hurt her seriously. If I had cared about her only a little, I should have kept what had happened a secret. Revealing all my shameful affairs in the name of honesty was nothing less than exhibiting myself as a disrespectable person with the intention that she should know it, and fundamentally, this meant that she was not so precious to me. If a secret is not kept where it belongs, it remains nothing but mere frivolity. Our generation is one without depth, failing to grasp the value of secrets, a generation existing within an information society based on the principle that every bit of information should be open, a society where, in the name of rationality, human emotions are killed. And I myself, having adjusted to that, was being the very egoist that I dislike most.

"Do it quickly, you bastard," Hyun-jae ordered, throwing her underwear in my face. At that, my penis stood up automatically, like some doll that had been switched on. As if exacting revenge, I embraced her hard, and without love or lotion, I did it.

Hyun-jae murmured, "I am shit." As if groaning, she continued to murmur, "I am shit, I am shit . . ."

And I murmured, in a slightly louder voice than Hyun-jae's, "I am a dog. I'm eating shit. I am a dog. I'm eating shit. I am a dog. I'm eating shit . . ."

In the profound depths of my sinking heart, a series of shivers gripped me, and I parted from Hyun-jae's body. The record had long finished playing, and a tingling silence like needles prickled our naked flesh. Hyun-jae lay on her belly, her skirt open, and I lay on my back, catching my breath and looking at the ceiling. If I had been able to smoke, I might have broken that silence, the longest of my life.

Finally breaking it herself, Hyun-jae said, "Your room is filled with pocket books."

"Everything we should read is in pocket books."

"They're also shit," she said, and out of all the books stacked up along the four walls in my attic room, she knocked over the pile directly in front of her. Like the sound of my heart breaking, the stack shattered to the floor.

Hyun-jae said, "You're an asshole."

From the nearby military base, a fighter plane took off, its roar shaking our brick-and-slate house. Into my attic room emptied of music, the roar of the jet engine surged, as anxious and annoying as experimental music. The roof of our house grew thinner every time a jet took off or landed. No thick roof could stop the noise from the newest jets. Any roof would get thinner.

As the jet's rumble dissipated into the distance, Hyun-jae rose stealthily and descended the stairs. And that was the end. As if the 16 days of the Olympic Games were a countdown to her death, the next day, the very day after the Games were over, she broke a 10th-floor window at the club that she liked to visit, in the building that her father might have built, and threw herself to the sidewalk below.

When I found out about her death in the local evening newspaper, the first thing to cross my mind was her underwear. I feel guilty about Hyun-jae, but the first thing that crossed my mind was the underwear that she had left behind in my attic room. I don't know if she'd left it intentionally or simply forgotten it, but after she'd gone down the stairs, I found her pink underwear, folded into a small shape resembling a carnation. Hyun-jae disliked putting on her underwear in front of me. Maybe she'd left it for that reason. No, maybe not. She could easily have carried it in her bag. Anyway, I had tossed it into a trash can because I couldn't imagine handing it over to her later, like some forgotten handkerchief.

Confronted with her death, my focusing only on the underwear felt very disrespectful, but it seemed a fitting symbol for our relationship, and that made me miserable. We got together just for the sex, not to seek love, not even that small amount of love needed to save each other. In her moment of despair, and in my meanness, I had led her to cut off all interest in me. I resolved not to cry. If I cried, neon would flow from my eyes.

Some might, perhaps, find it utterly banal and lacking in creativity that I actually dreamt of Hyun-jae that night. In my dream, her father was constructing the building even as Hyun-jae was breaking the club's window with her bare hands. Blood, her blood, gushed out. I woke from the dream, screaming, and could still see Hyun-jae, falling away toward the sidewalk, her bleeding hands reaching up to me.

Hyun-jae had once told me, "I don't know what to do. I should go to a university, but I'm not sure if I can."

"Do it step by step," I suggested.

"I am going down step by step on an escalator," she complained, "but my friends are rushing up frighteningly fast in an elevator. If this continues, I won't be able to make it into even a third-class university in Seoul."

That day, as we were riding the bus, heading for my attic room, she was in anguish about her falling grades. In fact, when I had first met Hyun-jae, her grades were already at the bottom and couldn't possibly drop further.

"A stupid girl," I thought. "There must have been many open windows, so why did she make such an effort to break that window and jump?"

Deep in the night, I awoke screaming, sat up, and sobbed. Fearful of the neon flowing from my eyes, I wiped them, then smelt and tasted the tears, but they had no smell or taste. Just regular tears. Relieved, I finally cried without restraint, sobbing, like Adam opening his eyes to a fake paradise. My Eve was a prostitute. My room was always dark and wet. If I sometimes opened the window to let out the foul smell of books, I saw the world under the neon crosses befouled with greater darkness and corruption than was in my room. Because the fake paradise to which my eyes had opened was so frightening, I sobbed loudly. My mother was awakened and came upstairs to my attic room.

"I'm sorry, Mother."

My mother patted my shoulder for a long time.

"I'll really start studying now."

I began to attend the cram school again. Thinking that I needed help only with English and Math while learning the other subjects on my own, I registered for those two subjects and studied the rest in my attic room. From then until exam day, worldly thoughts and doubts no longer plagued me.

Except once.

On the 16th of October that year, twelve inmates escaped from prison. Five of them had been cornered and had taken hostages. The dramatic events were being captured on TV for a live audience that very morning. After my math class, I sat in the cram school's restaurant, eating noodles and watching the hostage scene unfold. Someone who seemed to be the escaped prisoners' boss was wearing dark sunglasses and shouting out from the iron-barred window: "I'm a pessimist who wants to be a happy beggar. We tried to escape with dignity, controlling our sexual desires, but that was not the right thing to do. You policemen, how can you catch spies if you cannot catch us even with such a long cordon? It's a dirty world where money buys judges and executioners, you bastards. Get cars here by noon. We want to die in the fresh mountain air or in the cool river water. The poor become criminals, the rich become non-criminals. I am the last poet in the Republic of Korea."

Listening to this man, Ji Gang-hun, hurling such words for the TV cameras busily engaged in televising the lively scene, many people around me extolled him as a hero. He asked the police to play "Holiday" by the Bee Gees, but they played "Holiday" by the Scorpions instead. At that, the last poet in the Republic of Korea took a piece of glass and scratched a line across his throat. Some hours later, he was shot dead by a SWAT team. That incident struck me like a hard blow to the head. Some time before, I had felt the same headache. The previous year's presidential election had perplexed me in exactly the same way. If somebody wants to write a research paper on how the two Kims' failure to unify their pro-democracy campaigns affected the impressionable minds of high school students, I offer myself as research subject. Although I cannot demonstrate that I failed the university exam because of that election, I reacted more sensitively to the failed democratization campaign than other exam students did. And now, the prison escapees had thrown me into confusion again. What kind of world do I live in? Why is it in such chaos? I felt myself falling once more into a black hole. I needed to redirect my feelings. Otherwise, I would fall completely into that black hole and never emerge. I took out my math notebook and wrote the following words: "Reasons the five escapees, including Ji Gang-hun, are not heroes and their death no tragedy":

"We call someone a hero or his action a tragedy when he fights for justice and uses just methods but sustains a terrible defeat. The words 'hero' and 'tragedy' don't fit a struggle where the aim or method is unjust. If we look upon the five escapees with sympathy, we do so because some elements of their story can be called tragic. Their tragedy occurred when they used absurd methods to resist social absurdity. They tried to punish the world's immorality through their own crimes, an immoral method. The absurd society then showed them the yellow card of morality. That's why there was no other option for them than defeat. Their tragedy lay in not having correctly understood social ethics or the legal system's mechanisms. They therefore became the sort of heroes found in Hong Kong movies—or people like Rambo."

Even the most confusing thought can be organized when written in a notebook. Writing in a notebook, classifying things according to topics, and sticking a label on the cover for safekeeping can all help one understand any kind of confusion in the world and clarify the main point. On that day's evening news, the hostage drama's only survivor, Gang Young-il, was interviewed. He said that he and his friends had planned to escape to Taiwan or some other overseas country through the help of his girlfriend, a Taiwanese woman. How dramatic it was. If it had been a movie, people would have applauded them. Even the police would have put down their clubs or guns and enjoyed it. But it was not a movie; it was reality. If a movie hero were to come off the screen into reality, his on-screen actions would become criminal. The escapees didn't understand that. If they had wanted to become heroes, they should have gone to Hollywood. The film title could be *The Poor Become Criminals*, and the theme song would be the Bee Gees song "Holiday." This era's tough guy, the actor Lee Duk-hwa, would wear dark glasses and perform the lead role with enthusiasm. He would shout desperately, "The poor become criminals, the rich become non-criminals," and "I am the last poet in the Republic of Korea." And Ji Gang-hun and his comrades, the last romantic people of this era, would point their guns to one another's heads and pull the triggers. No, wait, to give full vividness to the art of tragedy, the film would do better to make use of real footage. The SWAT team in their camouflage uniforms would jump over the walls and fire their M16s randomly. Maybe thousands of shots. From Lee Duk-hwa's chest and head, red ketchup would flow down. The Bee Gees would be gloomily singing "Holiday": *de de de, de de de, de, de, de . . .*

The Poor Become Criminals becomes a hit, so the sequel, titled *The Rich Become Non-Criminals*, has already been planned. Its main character is Kim Gil-ho, one of the original twelve escapees, and he has not yet been caught. After changing his name and undergoing cosmetic surgery, he becomes a boss in the underworld, where he earns a lot of money. Retiring after becoming godfather of the underworld, he washes his hands of the criminal realm and enjoys his sunset years sitting in a big yard surrounded by his children and grandchildren. A police investigator, however, has been tracing him persistently and upon finding him reveals that he was one of the twelve who had escaped from prison years before. He is taken to court, but the judge declares him innocent. The rich become non-criminals! For the theme song, "Holiday" would also be fitting, the Bee Gees intoning with ridicule: *de de de, de de de, de, de, de . . .*

If a movie is a hit, it is usually followed by a stage adaptation. Then comes a documentary, followed by a photo book. No, the order can be different. Whether documentary, stage, movie or stage, documentary, movie, the order is not so important. What is important is how capitalism operates. Capital transforms any incident into something sensational and commercial. An entire industry is founded on a dirty incident, which drums up business, and a sequel is made. Capital ridicules meaning and renders it meaningless. When the incident has been sufficiently consumed, it is forgotten. In the search for other things of interest and developing them, truths like "the poor become criminals, the rich become non-criminals" aren't treated seriously and are no longer objects of research. As if nothing had ever happened.

Some days later, after all the escapees of the hostage drama had either died or gotten arrested, Chun Gi-hwan and Lee Chang-suk, among other family members of ex-president Chun Doo-hwan, were arrested one after another for bribery and other wrongdoings, but I was immersed in my studies. Summer and fall passed, and on the flyspecked wallpaper, more splotches appeared, the remains of swatted flies, mosquitoes, and other insects. At times, but only once in a while, I thought of Hyun-jae and remembered and sang a song about Paris she would sing when drunk.

We had once sung it the whole night through, changing Paris to New York, London, Hong Kong, Nice, LA. The song was "Paris I Cried For." And lowering our voices so that nobody could overhear, we traded Paris for Pyongyang, Kaesong, Hamhung, Chongjin, and Haeju among others, taking a pilgrimage of the Korean Peninsula, crying to think of those North Korean cities that we could not visit.

In the winter of that year, I took the exam and was initially unconcerned. I had set up a detailed plan to read through the pocketbooks of various publishing companies while awaiting the result, and I listened repeatedly to my favorite records. Also, I grew more interested in classical music and kept the radio channel on during classical music broadcasts. Yet, bands of the 50s and 60s still brought me more joy. Listening to them, I could hear Hyun-jae's voice.

The first time that we'd gone to the hotel, she told me, "I can only trust people who like the classics or traditional Rock and Roll. Contemporary music is disgusting."

As she'd said, the music these days, pouring from the radio every time you flicked one on, is disgusting, like trash. Rock music these days, sold as cheap bootlegs, is all corrupt. Bands sing crap like this:

> —My job's in killing (a hitman), and I have a good business.
> —God's love is a lie, so curse God instead.
> —If life's difficult, suicide is best.
> —Have sex with animals.

I could not help growing nervous as the year moved on and the day when the exam results were announced drew ever nearer. What if I had failed again? I was determined to enlist in the army if that happened. Was it going to be the university or the army? As the day steadily approached, the passing days began tormenting me. I took up smoking, started coughing dry coughs. To the old, stale-cookie smell of pocketbooks was added the reek of cigarette smoke.

Although I tried to dissuade my mother from coming along, telling her that I preferred to travel by myself to Seoul and see the result alone, she insisted on seeing her son's exam result as well. On a big shabby particleboard crudely set up for the posted results was my computer-printed exam registration number. Success. My mother gripped my hands tightly and shed tears. I hugged her, patting her on the back. The posting meant that I had secured a stepping stone to a higher rite of passage. My mother and I returned home on the evening bus. Riding south from Seoul to Daegu, my mother never released my hand, holding it the entire time.

The next morning, Eun-sun called me. "Adam, how did it go? Did you pass?"

I didn't answer.

"Did you fail?" she asked. "Oh, I know. You passed, right?"

Holding the phone to my ear, I didn't say a word. Later that day, we drank beer in a bar, and I listened to her tell me, without pausing, about being in prison the past summer and about the demonstration that she had joined, among other things, but my head just felt heavy.

"I stayed for less than a month in prison," she said, "A friend of my father, who has a high position, helped to get me released. I only needed to write that I regretted my actions."

Against the background music of a polka, she also read me a poem that she had written a few days before:

> I go to Las Vegas, to pick up dollars. I go to Texas, to grow marijuana. I go to the Pentagon, to make missiles. I go to Chinatown, to raise pigs. I go to LA, to become

> a homo. I go to Beverley Hills, to have a sex party. I go to Washington, D.C., to become a slutty secretary. I go to Soho, to take porno pictures. I go to San Francisco, to sell Chinese cabbage to Komericans. I go to Hawaii, to become a masseuse. I go to Hollywood, to meet Stallone. I go to New York, to scribble on the subway. I go to Detroit, to own a car wash. I go to El Paso, to fight the Mexicans. I go to Chicago, to get shot!

Finishing, she asked, "How does it sound? The title is 'Where are you going? America.'"

"It's not even as good as the lines of a pop song," I told her.

"It isn't?" she asked, then added, "That's really so, isn't it? People's poetry is like that."

Perplexed, I was speechless. Not for all the world could I understand what was in her mind. The moment that she finished talking, I slapped her cheek. "You believe that the poem you wrote is a people's poem!"

Eun-sun cried loudly, putting her head down on the table made from a big wooden wine barrel. "You don't know how much I suffer. I just want to die."

Eun-sun and I went to a motel to catch up on the lovemaking that we had missed for a year. It felt like returning to a house where I had lived before, where nothing was unfamiliar.

After making love, Eun-sun and I smoked, and she spoke again. "I managed to get into the university that I wanted and became a poet. But nobody treated me like a poet. When I went to a literary club to appear with pride as a woman poet, the indifference was worse. Adam, you know my vanity. Well, my vanity started to crumble. Everybody was reading only the poems of people's poets like Park No-hae, Paek Mu-san or Kim Nam-ju or Kim Ji-ha. Easy stuff, like for high school students. Moreover, they talked only about collective creation, ignoring someone like me."

Eun-sun continued talking sadly, like a woman in a bar lamenting her life. Gradually, I came to feel the suffering that she'd had to endure.

"People told me to get a new education," she revealed, "unless I wanted to become someone beyond saving. So, I joined a study group. I heard about things that I didn't actually care to understand, like a horse led to water that it doesn't want to drink. I wrote the poem "Land of Youth" during that time. Actually, I wasn't the only poet. Five or six people composed it collectively. The girl named Go Eun-sun was broken to pieces. In the academic realm, where I had arrived after studying hard for 12 long years from elementary to high school, all that I accomplished was ridding myself of myself."

She blew cigarette smoke up in the air, then put her cigarette out by stubbing it on the ash tray.

"I became part of the struggle merely by lending my name. One senior told me to treat it as a chance for the conversion that would root out my bourgeois disposition. You must have read about the rest in the newspaper. In one corner of the social section, my photo was shown gloomily like a woman spy. But how could I become a fighter and root out my capitalistic disposition merely by lending my name? How, when I was not really there? Forcibly deconstructed by their demagogy, where was the me who should think and reflect more independently? They pursued their accelerated movement with mere names and moral justification minus the active subjects. Adam, where is my true self?"

I felt so sorry for Eun-sun, and reached out to touch the cheek that I had slapped. To her question of how I had been doing, I replied that I had only been studying. I saw no need to speak of the other things.

"Adam," she said, "I will start anew. I will return to the time before my debut."

She and I stayed together that night, making love several

times. There are some plugs that are hard to put in and pull out and others that are too loose to put in tight, and so come out too easily, the electricity dying again and again. But we were ideal for each other. Even when our fingers touched, we were electrified.

"When is your registration?" she asked. "Should we travel to Seoul together?"

"No," I decided, "I'll go and register by myself."

In fact, to get to the point, I didn't register. When I went to Seoul with the registration fee, I again saw a forest of high-rise buildings, saw the crowd walking fast through the forest, and heard the sound of a familiar instrument. *Tschalang, tschalang* . . . On my way to the university with the fee money in my coat's inner pocket, the tambourine man came to mind. Smiling sweetly again and again, he said, "Look, you will become like me soon!" *Tschalang tschalang*. "You will go to the university, earn your grades, and graduate." *Tschalang, tschalang*. "The price is to occupy a desk in the building worth 50 trillion won. That's the end. You'll learn about computers, and your ability to process information quickly won't let you rest but will bury you in yet more work. You'll not find yourself able to rest more just because you are faster at processing information. You'll have to use your brain just as fast as the computer and train yourself to use computer functions automatically." *Tschalang, tschalang*. "In the end, you'll play the tambourine just like me. After becoming crazy, being crazy! Ha-ha, ha-ha!"

I had a headache looking at the buildings lined up one after another. The tambourine man was not alone. People, going and coming, busy among the buildings, all had tambourines in their hands. My ears felt ready to explode. More than one thousand tambourines were jangling together. Getting off the bus, I walked all day through the streets of Seoul. People were all strangers, and there was nobody whom I could talk to. Possessed by an urgent desire to talk to someone, I remembered the critic who had given the YMCA lecture. I went to a bookstore and called the publishing company that had published his book, asking how I could contact him.

A woman, apparently working in the office, said, "Mr. Lee has emigrated to America."

As if to ridicule me, the neon signs were glittering. From their hometown to Seoul, from Seoul to New York, people fly, riding on the acceleration. Would I ride at such a fast speed? If one cannot break the acceleration, one will fly out of the universe. NASA is doing it now. I went to a motel, a house always open and smiling to welcome us. I was hungry, and the sound of the tambourine had deafened my ears. I called room service and ordered some food, then after eating, I slept for a while, a dreamless sleep that I had not had for a long time.

When I woke up, the hour was not yet midnight. Maybe because I'd breathed in too much polluted air after walking around Seoul, there was a lot of sperm collected in my body, like trash that needed to be thrown out. I called the front desk again. After about half an hour, a woman came. She was cute and her name was Amy, but she was just called that and wasn't really a mixed person with Yankee blood.

We licked each other's wounds of desire. Although our desires were different, the difference was not so great. One buys the sex for money, and the other sells the sex for the same thing. If the wheel of fate turned, anybody could switch roles. I screwed my ennui, my condensed desire, into her vagina. I wanted to forget myself. I wanted to forget Seoul. Dripping with sweat, I tried to move my hips, but my consciousness became clearer, and Seoul became bigger. I could not come.

Unable to come in Seoul! I was sorry for Amy, who was trying so hard. Unable to come! It's enough to make one feel sorry for a prostitute. Several times, she sucked on my penis to help it get hard, but it would quickly fall limp again.

"Sorry," I said. "I'll try with my hand."

I masturbated while staring at her rear as she lay on her belly. After a while, the sperm that had collected deep down in my body like bits of hard metal came out and dirtied our naked bodies.

"It's because my mind is very tired," I explained, adding, "Sorry."

"No, you don't have to say anything," she told me. "I can understand that feeling."

I paid her more. "If you don't want to sleep here, you can go."

"That's okay," she said. "Tonight, I want to sleep and relax."

Crying into my pillow, I murmured the lyrics of Bob Dylan's "Knocking on Heaven's Door."

The next morning, I washed her body and hair, and in the room, I dried her body with a towel, even cleaning the parts between her toes. We had breakfast. I wanted to treat her to something nice in a good restaurant, but she insisted on a simple meal in a fast-food restaurant. We had just a hamburger and Coke, along with a few pieces of Kentucky Fried Chicken.

"It's over for someone like me if I get fat and old," she explained.

I nodded. It was the last day for registration, but I decided to return home immediately. Against my protests, she accompanied me to Seoul Station to wave goodbye as I went through the gate.

"Usually, I watch movies during the daytime," she told me, "and whenever I see lovers saying goodbye at a train station or an airport, I cry, wishing that it could happen to me."

She bought a flower bouquet from a shop, and in front of the gate, she held it out to me. "Only lovers can truly say goodbye," she said, "and I have never loved someone until now. I cannot ask just anyone to say goodbye to me. When I first saw you last night, I thought you might understand."

With two hands, I accepted the bouquet she was holding. I

felt odd and embarrassed, but because of her, I was encouraged that one can love with the heart of a prostitute and build a new world. Deep in my heart, I thanked her.

"Doesn't it hurt your pride to be seen off by a prostitute?" she wondered.

"Not at all," I replied in a genuinely respectful tone, and I hugged and kissed her for so long that all the women standing in front of the gate must have grown jealous. I then lost myself in the crowd gathering at the gate. The last thing that I saw in Seoul was her pure smile and the 63 Building standing high and lonely like my penis that wouldn't ejaculate even though it was erect.

Riding third-class, which was extremely slow and bumpy, and saying to myself, "Go back to your hometown," I indulged myself, wondering if I could do something greater than going to university, like become a literary translator, or work as a literary critic. Could I perhaps become a writer? Writing would be painful. That would mean breaking the acceleration of the world with my entire body, and to do that would require me to endlessly reflect on the meaning of my existence.

Through writing, I would be able to enjoy the "pain of creation" that I had desired so much. That pain could be used to find my way back to the lost paradise, the reality, the truth, allowing me to firmly reject the fake paradise. Two efforts would be necessary to regain that reality lost to the fake paradise. First, I should not overestimate my reasoning abilities, I should limit my freedom. Humility would be necessary for this. And second, because a good world cannot be made easily, I should not give up if I didn't see it forming clearly soon. For that reason, perseverance would be needed. Humility and perseverance were virtues required not only of me, who wanted to write, but also for anyone who dreamed of a better world despite living in the paradise of acceleration.

Back in Daegu, I bought a used typewriter. I had always thought that I needed a typewriter, and at the age of 20, I finally got one. I will now be able to write something with it. Letters or a journal, or maybe something creative. And if I write a novel, I will begin by depicting the portrait of my 19th year this way:

> I was nineteen years old, and the things that I most wanted to have were a typewriter, prints of Munch's paintings, and, for playing records, a turntable to hook up to a cassette player's speakers. Those things alone were all that I wanted from this world when I was nineteen.

The Seventh Day

A lot of words were first necessary before two people could lie down together, just as there were words at the beginning of the world.

But now, they don't utter a word. The man and the woman are taking off each other's clothes in silence. Nobody speaks, not a word. The small room, bright with sunlight, hard and sharp like fragile glass, is filled with silence only, and the clothes, removed with effort from each other's bodies, are falling to the dry floor with rustling like whispers, as if all the words they'd uttered are breaking off their bodies.

Before the two lay down naked, a lot of words were first necessary, breathtaking confirmation and oath, and doubts, like "I love you," "Do you love me?" "I want to be loved" . . .

The clothes lost their authority, piece by piece. While removing the clothes from each other's bodies, the two were under the illusion that they were taking off hard tinplate sheets. Or it might have been the hypocrisy they had covered themselves with through words. Regardless, whenever one piece of clothing after another was removed by the other's lightly trembling fingers, the two felt themselves freed, a fresh feeling.

Out the window, the sea looked as if it were covered with a blue slate roof. The two looked at each other's dazzling bodies, the first man and the first woman, made completely naked by their own hands. There was no fear, neither was there shame. Their trembling fingers had trembled less the more pieces of clothing were removed, and the two grew peaceful gazing at each other's bodies. Outside the window, a hill like a blue slate roof was shimmering. The two were watching the blue hill breaking and rolling. Naked, they were standing.

After a while, the man sought the woman's hands and locked his ten fingers with her ten fingers. Like a scene in many movies. His lips then covered her lips, so a novelist might write. The tongues in their mouths began to move. They moved hotly, softly, finely. The two slowly lay down on the floor. Lying there, the man and woman watched a flock of waterfowl soaring up outside the window.

The man stroked the woman's soft skin up and down, and the woman touched the man's smooth back. Their flesh was tender, like that of children, and smelt fragrant, and was honest like the heart of a child. Each body lightly trembled, unfolded, folded, stretched, or hardened, as the other's hand touched it. They caressed each other so thoroughly in every nook and cranny that they seemed like two blind people competing urgently to read ever faster a book in Braille. The two were Braille books for each other, blind people desiring to read the signs written on each other's bodies. But the two were one book, divided into two volumes and not separate books.

Given this, it is especially significant that their chance meeting was brought about by a book. On that day, the two had met in a bank downtown. The man was pushing buttons for his pin code, after inserting his online cash card into an ATM machine. When he had finished pressing the four numbers, derived from the date of his birth, the screen flashed instructions for him to type in the amount of money needed. The man pressed those buttons, then the one for confirmation. From deep inside the ATM, strange sounds of working machinery could be heard, as if a servant were whispering to a master, "Yes, master! Yes, master!"

Just a few minutes earlier, the woman had also entered the bank. She was holding a book to her chest, a red book that was neither too thick nor too thin. This book, like a name tag on the chest of an elementary school child, imbued her with a specific character. Quietly standing behind the man and waiting for him to finish, she asked a guard who happened to pass if she could use a card from a different bank. Only then, upon hearing a very resonant voice, did the man turn around and look at her. He saw the profile of a woman's face, a surprisingly ordinary face. Yes, too ordinary to catch his attention. Instead, his eyes were distracted by the red book held to her chest. Later, he would be able to scrutinize her face.

After a long caress, the woman's face flushed red. And the man? In sex scenes, most novels pay more attention to describing the woman's body than the man's. And they pay more attention to describing the inner state of the man than of the woman. As if the woman were simply the man's other self. Of course, the writer of this story will do the same. Unconsciously, his pen will crawl on her naked body as if drawing a nude sketch: The woman's body seemed weak but opulent, the skin like a white gem, and out of the small lips, opened like a pomegranate, came low sighs, almost inaudible, as the woman's body grew hot, and out of the small mute mouth between the legs, some bodily fluid was flowing like sighs . . . etc.

Holding her waist tightly, the man twisted his genitalia, now incorporating his whole body, into her genitalia now encompassing her entire existence. What kinds of explanation are needed here? About the sexual intercourse of man and woman, explained so often and in such detail? The two didn't speak at all. As if afraid that the joy flowing from their bodies might be heard, they clenched their teeth and gathered back the sighs they'd just uttered, but they kept their ears wide open, as if taking care not to waste them.

They were talking through their flesh. Their pores were fusing together across their entire bodies, everywhere, and their two mouths, both the upper and lower ones, were also merged. They could say nothing, and needed to say no words. Still, they shared words without speaking. The many words that they had shared with each other so far had slipped away as sighs through their teeth. The many lies and the exaggerated, commonly held beliefs about love and sex were just onomatopoeic words making sounds. "Do you remember the day we first met?"

On precisely that day, she could not use a different bank's ATM card due to some problem in the network link between the two banks. An expression of disappointment flickered briefly on the woman's face. But because the disappointment crossed her face so lightly, nobody else would have readily noticed. At that moment, the man's requested cash whirred from the machine. Evening had nearly arrived, and the banks downtown were drawing down the shutters at their main entrances. The man and woman were walking side by side down the not very lengthy hall leading to the rear emergency exit. On the way to the bank's back door, the man had a strong desire to say something to the woman. What might it be? After thinking of several lines of dialogue, the novelist writes:

"Miss, you're reading the same book as me."

The woman, pausing to linger, looked at the man who had just spoken. The man, smiling almost imperceptibly, took a book from under his arm and showed it to her. The book still had the bookstore's special, protective paper covering folded over its spine and covers. The man did a double take and opened the cover with a long, thick finger. Then, she smiled, and even that smile was merely an ordinary one on an ordinary face.

In the thin, narrow hall that was like a water pipe leading to the back door, the two smiled at each other, showing each other their books like secret signs. The man asked, "Would you mind if

I spent the money I withdrew on you?"

The woman again smiled the ordinary smile on her ordinary face, or so wrote the novelist . . .

The sunlight, entering through the window, streamed down in layers through the room emptied of even a chair and gathered around the two naked bodies as if fawning over them, and the sound of the waves, as sharp as that from shaking a sack filled with blue stone shards, flowed unceasingly into the room from outside. Her climax didn't come easily. No virgin finds climaxing easy in her first experience. Except that this is a porno novel. Like a viscous fluid congealing with time, the two became solid, their motions slowing down. Here, the climax of the two had to be postponed a bit longer.

For some time now, a man and a woman talking about sex during their first meeting has become nothing special at all. Unlike earlier times, when one had to talk about sex with authority and deal with it in a rather scholarly way to avoid any needless misunderstanding, talking about sex has now become an everyday affair, something public that people discuss with no reluctance. People now talk about sex as if talking about the scores from the previous evening's baseball game. Of course, the dialogue of the two characters will become more sophisticated due to the nature of the book that brought them together.

"This book entices people to buy it through the erotic cover design, which fits the title," he noted, "and it enhances readers' desire to read it because this is the first time this French author has been published in Korea."

"That's right," she agreed. "This author was published here a bit late, and that's probably because he's unclassifiable. The books already written about sex can generally be put into either of two categories—excluding the dirty, commercial, unserious attempts. One category lifts the sexual act to the level of a ritual in esoteric Buddhism, describing the experience as spiritual ecstasy. In such books, the sensation of the body that has freed itself from the dark pool of desire becomes in turn a focus for meditation on the mystery of creation and reincarnation. The other kind of book, opposed to this perspective, starts from a position that dismisses such mysticism. Essentially, it treats sex, whether hidden or open, as an object for strict and objective analysis in the name of science. Books of the first sort take the view that sex is more than we experience, whereas books of the second sort deal with fewer things than we experience. Both present extreme, abstract views of sex. The reason for the delay in translating this author was probably because he didn't take either position."

The two were exchanging their opinions about the same book, which they had just read, as they sat in a corner of a cozy, relaxing café. They kept their coffee cups on the table between them, and the man, who had been taking sips of coffee and water alternately, expanded on the woman's words as soon as she had finished.

"I agree with you," he said. "In fact, almost all his writings are too rational to be describing individual mystical experience but also rely too much upon inner instincts to be an objective report. He firmly insists not only that science has objectified eroticism beyond understanding but also that any scientific method of investigation into eroticism is to be distrusted because inner experience, the essential and inexplicable characteristic of eroticism, cannot be approached that way. He criticizes the *Kinsey Report* because the researchers used statistics to understand the sexual act, and he doesn't completely agree with Levi Strauss's approach through structural anthropology, which tries to find the rules of the collective mind's unconscious. His view, between the two poles of the objective and the subjective, without coming down on either side, is a product of tension and conflict that tries to understand life as discontinuity in continuity and continuity in discontinuity."

Let's return to the place where the two were just recently postponing their climax. If we forget and ignore them for too long, they might become a couple of fossilized bodies, one stacked upon the other. After a long rest restoring their energy, the two have started again to rush toward climax, having gone from slow motion to a stop, their genitalia stuck to each other. The sighs from the woman's small lips and the rough breaths from deep within the man's lungs seem to definitely prevent their becoming petrified fossils. But what is a sexual climax?

"At the peak of eroticism," he remarked, "one is no longer aware of one's sexual partner, not even of the other's existence. One even forgets the biological drive to preserve the species. In eroticism's fulfillment through a sexual climax, one focuses only upon oneself. In that sense, the inner experience that he emphasizes seems to have something to do with real existence."

At that moment, the woman, because she had not yet experienced sex, could not express her complete agreement. It would take a long time for her to understand that at the peak of sexual intercourse, one is conscious only of oneself, regardless of whether the sexual act starts from the instinct for species-preservation or from love for the other, and she had thus had to wait until this present moment.

The flesh speaks. Give me some more! Please me a bit more! Satisfy me a bit more! In this moment, there is only me! In that way, each forgot the other's existence. From the beginning, there was no drive for species preservation. The flesh knew it already. To establish myself, I have to have an antithesis! For the one to reach climax, the other also has to reach climax! For the climax is namely a collapse, a state of suspended animation, death.

"Eroticism is life that burrows into death," the man continued, "for life gives birth to new life through death. The very act of life that imprints death upon birth is the act of procreation. We can find a clear example in the unicellular animal undergoing asexual reproduction. When this simple unit of life divides into two, the original cell disappears and exists simultaneously. For humans, the moment of division becomes inner experience through 'loss of consciousness.'"

In this way, the two experienced that existential dangling, that state of suspended animation, that loss of consciousness, and that brief moment of death, and in the meantime, a dark curtain dropped slowly down to cover the red sun that had been heating a corner of the day. Very soon, stars were pouring forth like sand spilt from a jar, and a crescent moon like a yellowish pot was moving around trying to catch them.

The first night in the small bungalow on the coast passed, and the second day came. The two slept until the sun had climbed to high noon, shrinking in size and casting small shadows upon the earth. On the windowsill, a few gulls had flown down to rest and were mewling, glancing furtively at the naked bodies of the man and the woman. "*Scree, scree, scree, scree, scree, scree* . . ." It was the woman who woke up first. Awake, she inspected closely the face of the man still deep asleep. She then let her eyes run down to gaze at his groin. It was so shrunken that it appeared somehow distorted. If someone pointing to the man's genitals had noted that it was all intended for sex, how disappointing might that have been for her? The man's genitals, shrunken to an ill-appearing afterthought, seemed to caricature the previous day's romance, which had taken all day long, so much time it was almost tedious.

The woman put her hand upon his crotch and touched the sagging scrotum. Touched by her fingertips, it wriggled the way a small, living octopus does. Motivated by a strong curiosity, she continued to touch his sac with the one hand while beginning to work up his penis from base to tip with the other hand, all the time lying closely next to him, her legs alongside his torso. As the man's penis started to grow hard, the woman sat up and, sitting next him, put her head between his legs. A powerful animal odor, smelling distantly of stabled horses or cattle, rose from his groin, which was slightly wet with a mixture of sweat, urine, and sperm, among other things, and made her dizzy. The woman inhaled deep into her lungs, drawing in the scent more fully.

The strong masculine odor from his groin rose from her nostrils to her brain and then spread in pungent waves throughout her whole body. Again, she felt dizzy. Taking several more deep breaths, she mouthed his scrotum, probing it with her tongue. The sac was soft, and she greedily drew the entire scrotum into her mouth, rolling the testicles. Immediately, the man's penis stood up hard, though slightly tilted, like the Leaning Tower of Pisa. The thought occurred to the woman that a man is two-faced. If the man had been able to hear and respond to her thought, he would have said, "Yes, you are right." The woman moved her lips up and licked the tip of his penis with her tongue. The sleeping man's other self, wanting to enjoy itself alone without the sleeping man, stood up more erect on its own, extending itself long, dark, and straight. Every man has another man in his body that expresses itself independent of his will. The woman took as much of it into her mouth as possible, from the top down the shaft, and nodded. Her actions brought a new feeling, one that she had never felt before. But let's not call it what women sense when they experience the feeling of motherhood, as during a pregnancy, when they bear a fetus in their wombs, for that would not describe how it affected her to have a man's most valuable part in her mouth . . .

Charmed into a relaxed feeling of rapture, the man opened his eyes and discovered the reason for his rapture. She was pressing his genitals tightly between her small lips. The man stretched his arm to stroke the woman's neck, and her hair rubbed against his groin. The woman felt sad, on the one hand, that she had lost one man, but was satisfied, on the other hand, that she had awakened the other man from his deep sleep, through her efforts to unite his soul and his body. She tossed her head to flip her hair from her face, so the man could better see what she was doing. Her mouth was red and wet as it had been the previous night, when he had desired it intensely for so long. The man thinks that every woman has, like a prostitute, several holes, several vulvas.

After watching her for quite a long time, he took her two ankles and pulled the lower part of her body up onto his chest and started licking her vulva, which was now near his face. From its warm opening, her body's fluid flowed slowly, smooth like rain but tasting as soft and rich as cream soup. Her hips, as she was probed by his tongue, jerked and turned erratically, as if stung by a bee. Hasn't this classical position, called the 69, been so graphically depicted in so very many porno films? It would be acceptable for the writer to leave off describing this scene.

The man, though struggling to delay ejaculation just a bit longer, lost control so quickly that his sperm suddenly gushed forth. The woman downed this sensual fluid, swallowing drop by drop, and the semen slid down the slippery length from her mouth through her throat to her stomach. Enthusiasts like to measure the quantity of semen an average man releases, what sorts of organic matter it consists of, and how many calories it has.

Gulping down the warm sperm, the hunger she had felt from the moment of her waking was instantly satisfied, and she felt sated and languid. Unexpectedly, she started hiccupping. Her hiccupping after drinking the sperm of a man awakened so late in the morning struck the woman as somehow touching. While hiccupping, she stroked his withering penis from its root up to the top of its head with her five long, thin fingers as if milking a goat. But the penis, being stingy, allowed only a few drops of semen to be squeezed out. She put her tongue out to each drop and accepted the sensual fluid as though swallowing valuable drops of honeydew, and her expression had an oddly pious cast, as if she were swallowing some sacred, 100-carat diamond. Even then, she fumbled with his scrotum several times, as if to assure herself she'd missed nothing, and milked his penis again from root to head, taking each dewdrop of scarce semen and finally licking the thin film of glistening, sensual fluid from her lips.

The man's penis, after its prickling seizure, had withered as suddenly as if a nerve had been cut. But the woman, who now wanted sexual intercourse through every hole in her body, didn't accept the withering. She pressed against the man's withered genitalia with her thin wrist, its blue veins showing through transparent skin, while the man, enervated from his overpowering orgasm, utterly exhausted, watched her hand moving as it masturbated him.

How much time passed? The man's withered genitals unexpectedly began to revive and soon stood up hard again, and the man, unable to control his desire to come, stood up quickly, gripped her hair roughly, turned her face to the side, and poured his semen first into one ear and then into the other, dividing it properly. At that moment, the woman felt herself in a warm sea. The semen, overflowing from her two ears, moved whenever she turned her head, and it dampened all sound until it had dried in her ears like an old crust and crumbled there.

All day long, she accepted the man's semen, opening for him every hole in her body, and the man enjoyed each one, and the whole experience was quite pleasing for both. When the man ejaculated into her nose, the semen flowed through the nostrils into her throat, making her sneeze and laugh, and when he ejaculated into her eyes and rubbed her open eyes with the palm of his hand so that the semen would soak into the retinas, she felt thrilled to think that she might go blind. In fact, as the semen sank into her eyes, covering the retinas, they grew cloudy as if eye-drops had been put in, and the man's image shimmered, dissolving into two or more figures before her eyes.

The holes on the woman's face sensed the man with their own powers of taste, smell, hearing, and seeing, and if the holes could become pregnant like a womb, for example, if her eyes' pupils could absorb the man's sperm and be fertilized, her eyeholes would have given birth to countless other eyeballs as slimy as tadpole eggs after nine months of gestation. Pretty eyeballs resembling her pupils.

The man, wrung dry as clothes that had been spun in a washer-dryer, lay as if knocked out and was stretched out along the same line as the sun now lying on the horizon. He had ejaculated onto the woman countless times and had rubbed the semen elaborately over her whole body as if spreading on body oil so that it had soaked deeply into her skin through the pores. "No more, I can't any more, I am not a dog!" he wanted to cry out but had no energy left even for screaming. Sensing his condition, the woman thrust her hips before his face, prostrating herself on her arms and feet. Her anus, the final hole, was quivering as if to gulp down the entire universe.

"Sexual deviation and anomaly among lovers doesn't correspond to the world's definitions of sadism and masochism," the woman said. "If I should someday love a man, I will let him taste everything of me. I will allow him to flog my back and hips with his belt and let him release anything from his body onto my body. I will even submit my anus to him until it gets ruined."

"But still," he demurred, "I wouldn't like to do it through the anus. It might not fit my taste . . . Right, it looks so dirty, and it is not very different from sadism because it treats a woman shamefully."

"We should distinguish between an act performed for true love and an act of crude sadism," she said. "True love between a man and a woman may mean ridding themselves of the shame between them, of the ugliness in the meaning of shameful acts, one after another. True love may make them love even those ugly, shameful parts. If one loves the other truly, one would want to taste everything of the other. And that would be a good way to confirm their love for each other, wouldn't it?"

"That's the logic of sadism," he observed. "Their actions are all done under the excuse of confirming love, but in fact, love for sadists is just rhetoric for justifying a deviant desire that they can't control. Sadists need the abused object out of desire and not out of love."

The conversations between the two in the city always began with them talking about sex and ended with them defining sex. For them, no topic other than sex existed, almost as if no conversation were necessary unless it was about sex. Sex was their only material for communication.

"Don't convict de Sade so much," she admonished. "The author of the red book that made our meeting possible suggested that de Sade was the only person who approached eroticism's fulfillment, and for him, this very same de Sade was considered to have nearly transcended 'taboo' and 'violation.' Oddly, people take the acts that the Marquis de Sade had projected into transcendence and put them back into the category of taboo, but if possible, we should make people leap over the taboo that people condemn as sadism and violation. It's not true that there is no way. As you have just shown through your worry, and as I had said before, if we don't degrade the other as object and thing but approach 'sadism' with true love for each other, we could make 'sadism' null and overcome it."

The man hesitated, then asked, "And what's the end result of that? Is the end not, perhaps, death?"

When the man penetrated her anus deeply with his penis like the point of a spear hardened with the difficulty of forging a knife edge, the woman spread out on the floor and wept sadly enough to arouse sympathy. Outside, the many birds cried an earful, *zeet, zut, zeet, zut, zeet, zut . . .*, and gathered in the sky along the coast, like stars of the deaf, the mute, and the blind.

The next day at noon, the two were sitting face to face, very properly on the sandy plain of the empty coast, their clothes lying nearby. Where had all the birds flown? The sky, as if drawn by an elementary school child, was blue and empty apart from the blazing one-eyed sun.

After flattening the gently curved sandy plain with their hips to render it more comfortable for a long sitting, the two looked into each other's eyes. The gentle sea breeze passed by, tickling their faces. The two relaxed their shoulders. As if desiring to waste no energy . . . the two waited . . . looking into each other's eyes for some several minutes, until the man nodded. The nodding was so subtle that it would scarcely have been noticeable if they had not previously alluded to it in a promise, but the alert woman, who had adroitly caught his nod, herself nodded in response. Releasing a deep sigh, she slowly lifted her right arm and slapped him straight across his left cheek. Although prepared, the man's head turned slightly, because she slapped harder than he had expected. After slapping his cheek, the woman's expression remained unchanged, indifferent. Twisting his head back, the man felt relief deep in his heart when he saw the indifference on the face of the woman who had slapped him. Although unlikely, if he had seen embarrassment or surprise on her face, he would have been unable to continue this game. Now the man slowly lifted his left hand. The woman was gazing into the eyes of the man whose left hand was raised to the level of his shoulder, and her pupils dilated with curiosity. Suddenly, in the blink of her eye, his thick palm slapped against her right cheek. Her head, shifted slightly to one side by the slap, turned back.

The waves ceased their heart-like beating. Instead of the sound of waves, the coast was now filled with resounding slaps continuing slowly all day long. The woman's cheeks were bruised blue and beautiful, and the man's were so completely swollen that they were distorted, even drooping. They had started, bit by bit, with their shoulders and arms relaxed, but over time, they had to slap each other's cheeks with all their strength as they reached the inevitable limits of their diminishing powers.

Around sunset, the woman, whose hands were hurting, suddenly stood up and kicked the man's belly. The man rolled on the sandy ground, groaning from the sudden attack, while the woman, kneeling at his head, watched his body's violent convulsions. After some time, the man overcame his pain, got up from the ground where he had been stretched out, and with all his might kicked the belly of the woman, who had been kneeling at his head, watching his suffering. In turn, he kneeled at her head, deliberately staring into her face, distorted by pain, and at her body with its delicate, vibrating convulsions. The woman, after rolling and groaning for a long time, raised herself up and kicked his belly. Again, the man . . .

Fortunately for them, the moon was very bright that night, and they were able to dig their sadistic passion into one another's flesh for a long time. Only when completely exhausted, unable to move even a single finger, did they finally fall asleep on the sandy ground, stretched out to their full lengths. For those two, who had exercised their sadism and masochism alternately upon each other all day, there was no energy left for returning to the bungalow, for they could no longer move their limbs at will.

They had not planned how to spend the fourth day on the coast. Why? From fear? No, they had believed that if they had a plan for three days, the remaining days would work themselves out automatically without any plan. If their plan for the first three days worked out, it would activate the other days.

The fourth sun rose. The two could not even move their bodies until the sun had climbed high in the sky. Although awake early, their bodies wouldn't move. Lying on the beach, the two looked up at the sky through horribly swollen eyes. The sea, which had seemed hard as marble the day before, was rocking with waves breaking into smaller wavelets like the breaking of grinding glass. From torn, swollen lips, the woman spoke.

"There," she meant to say. "Look over there. A hang glider."

But in fact, she didn't finish the whole sentence, for the man sprinkled a handful of sand over her face and cried, "That tongue! Tongue!"

The man then pulled the belt from his nearby pants and started sharpening the tin buckle on a stone half hidden in a hollow of the sand.

Meanwhile, the hang glider, trailing a long tail, was sinking down below the horizon, as if trying to escape to a different world.

The man, having sharpened the buckle, pulled the woman's tongue down to the stone and cut it at the root. Red blood poured in full drops upon the stone, and the long scream of the woman made the waves, climbing toward the shore, vibrate slightly. The man threw the woman's severed tongue onto the sand and then put his own tongue, stretched out fully, onto the bloodstained stone. This time, the woman took his tongue, protruding and stretched out to its full length on the stone, and severed it with the sharpened buckle. She then put the bloody tongue immediately into her mouth and chewed it. It was the most tender, chewy food that she had ever eaten, and it was the only food she'd had for days.

The man, watching her chewing his own tongue, looked for hers. It had been tossed onto the sand, and was already totally covered with flies and ants. He picked it up, washed it roughly in the seawater, and squatted, pushing it into his anus. This act of putting food for the mouth into an anus was as impressive as the high Buddhist monks' cry of "*Hal!*" Being soft, however, it slipped out again and again, only tickling his anus more softly than tissue, and without another's help, the tongue seemed unable to enter his anus.

The woman watched the man's dimwitted act, which seemed intended to imitate, in its own ridiculing way, her act of swallowing his tongue. But she soon changed her mind because his sweaty effort, like one squatting to answer the call of nature under the hot sun, appeared beautiful and touching. So, she summoned all her remaining strength and returned to the bungalow, brought back one of her high-heeled shoes, had him lie on his belly, and used the tip of the high heel to push her own tongue deep into his anus.

"Have you ever read a porno novel written by this man?" he had asked her in the café on the day of their first meeting, tapping the red book that had enabled their encounter. "There's an amazing one where the main character, a woman, tore out a Catholic priest's eye and used it to masturbate." Noticing the expression on her face, he asked, "What? Is that disgusting?"

"No, not that," she said. "I was thinking of a porno novel from another country that quite impressed me. There was a man who felt joy only through suffering at the hands of a woman. Once, as the man was lying naked on his belly, the woman trod in high heels from his neck down his back to his buttocks and put the tip of her high heel into his anus, driving him crazy with pleasure."

As the woman's severed tongue filled his anus completely, the man felt comforted, satisfied. During that time hang gliders flew in thick flocks over the sea, most of them sinking into its waves, with only a few flying on beyond the horizon. Over the sea, there were evergreens, green for the whole year, and people who sang while lying under the trees and slept for a whole day . . . But could such a paradise ever exist? How could our clear, reasonable minds understand that such a part of the world might continue to exist in isolation after the other part had collapsed? And wouldn't that paradise itself collapse, if such a real paradise did exist beyond the sea, different than our part of the world here, if the truly good people lived there? Because those people who had reached that paradise would criticize themselves and break down from guilt for this world and for the people on this side whom they could not save because of their own goodness.

At the moment, the woman, who had been lying on the shore and watching the hang gliders flying over the sea, turned to glance at the man, who, exactly like her, was lying and watching the hang gliders. He shed a tear, and his face revealed a desire to fly off with them, if only he had possessed wings.

"How selfish to think of escaping to the other world in the midst of witnessing that this world is falling apart, and to believe that he alone is qualified to enter the other world!" thought the woman, seeing in his tears the man's selfish ego. Averting her eyes from him, and disgusted by his weak, shameful conduct, she pulled the bloodstained stone from the sand, and mercilessly brought it down on top of both of his feet and ankle bones. The man took the stone from her, broke her two white kneecaps, and after a long deliberation, removed the bones from inside her knees. "Now," she thought, "we will not be able to escape to a better place than here." The last hang glider flying across the sky disappeared beyond the horizon as the sun went down.

The fifth day. The two awoke at sunrise and dragged themselves along the sandy ground. They found stone pieces that could be used as knives, and all day long, they sharpened them on a rock at the shore.

"As a cultural animal," the man had said, "a human being simultaneously possesses an inner desire for work and reason on the one hand, and an inner desire for chaos and violence on the other hand. Labor and reason make life possible, but in a worldview limited by human reason, they trap the human being and even isolate him as an individual. Violence and chaos eventually cause that individual's death, but these also break the individual border imposed by reason and herald a world guaranteed by the life linking individuals or linking humans and nature. It is taboo that protects labor from violence, but it is through violation that we are able to access both worlds, using the elastic force of taboo. We could say that eroticism is a participation in this violation through the sexual act, or through similar acts."

"The fulfillment of eroticism means simultaneously transcending the two most powerful taboos that trap humans, namely, the taboos of death and sex," she said. "Anyway, we have both come to the same conclusion through this book. This is really something unusual. Yet, I am not sure if our agreement corresponds to the author's intention."

"Oh, that's an unnecessary worry," he replied. "Misreading is the fate of an author and the right of every reader. And the author of this book was born with more of this fate than any other author. However you read the book, it is dedicated to your inner experience."

It was hard work sharpening a stone weapon from a blunt one. The two momentarily fell asleep from exhaustion, but after soon awakening, they hurried to sharpen their stones further, testing the points of the sharpened stones against their fingertips. The two humans, bruised blue across their entire bodies, dragging themselves on their belly like sea turtles and pulling two loose legs around in the sands formed a scene so unusual that it seemed not to belong to this earth. Meanwhile, the sun of the fifth day sank below the waves.

The next day, even before the sun had arisen, the hearts of the two had started to beat with excitement. For real perfection, the two had decided to sharpen their stones some more, and throughout their anxious activity, time flew by like an arrow. Near evening, thunder and lightning began to tear the sky, but this seemed to presage no rain.

The man waited after he'd finished his sharpening, but the woman had already long finished and was making the sharpened knife ever sharper with the meticulousness and eye for detail typical of women. To pierce the heart properly, it would seem better to proceed before the sun set. The man approached the woman. It was hard to approach her little by little, dragging his worn-out body. The woman, taking a deep breath, remained in her place, like a bride awaiting her bridegroom. The man thought she was as beautiful as a flower though she was crippled, bruised and torn. He felt like Ulysses returning to Penelope after many trials.

With her left arm, the woman grasped the left shoulder of the man who had exerted himself so painfully to crawl over to her, and the man grasped her right shoulder with his right arm. As the woman plunged her stone knife into his heart, the man plunged his own stone knife, held in his right hand, deep into her heart.

Their actions took place almost simultaneously, and at the moment when the stone knives pierced their hearts—no, at the very moment when they each plunged a stone knife into one another's hearts, the man and the woman declared their love to each other, with their severed tongues, in words that nobody could have understood:

> "*Oh! Ah ov ooh!*"
> "*Oh! Ah ov ooh!*"

Though no one else could have understood, these two understood the truth and each other's appeal, shouted with their short tongues . . .

Late on the morning of the seventh day, the day of rest, an airplane was crossing over the sea, scattering the low-lying rainclouds. It was a bomber fully loaded with nuclear weapons, and as the hazy sun looked down on the beach from the high sky, the two had become stone pillars, hugging each other in sitting positions like cripples, and they looked good, so peaceful and holy . . . (Amen).

* The "red book" mentioned in this story is *Eroticism* by Georges Bataille, and the dialogues between the man and woman of the story are quoted from the book reviews of Jo Han-kyung and Jang Jung-il. The pornographic novel written by Bataille is *The Story of the Eye*.

Jang Jung-il was born in 1962. Once he began his career as an author, the self-educated Jang's wide-ranging tastes led him to try his hand at various genres. Jang Jung-il is infamous—and has even been jailed—for his erotic and violent fiction. He continues to write, albeit with less controversy, given Korean society's increasing liberality.

Hwang Sun-Ae and Horace Jeffery Hodges live in Seoul, Korea, and have co-translated several works of Korean literature together. Hwang Sun-Ae has a doctorate in German literature from the University of Munich, Germany, and works as a freelance translator. Horace Jeffery Hodges has a doctorate in history from UC Berkeley, and works as a professor at Ewha Womans University and as an editor.

The Library of Korean Literature

The Library of Korean Literature, published by Dalkey Archive Press in collaboration with the Literature Translation Institute of Korea, presents modern classics of Korean literature in translation, featuring the best Korean authors from the late modern period through to the present day. The Library aims to introduce the intellectual and aesthetic diversity of contemporary Korean writing to English-language readers. The Library of Korean Literature is unprecedented in its scope, with Dalkey Archive Press publishing 25 Korean novels and short story collections in a single year.

The series is published in cooperation with the Literature Translation Institute of Korea, a center that promotes the cultural translation and worldwide dissemination of Korean language and culture.

SELECTED DALKEY ARCHIVE TITLES

MICHAL AJVAZ, *The Golden Age.*
The Other City.
PIERRE ALBERT-BIROT, *Grabinoulor.*
YUZ ALESHKOVSKY, *Kangaroo.*
FELIPE ALFAU, *Chromos.*
Locos.
IVAN ÂNGELO, *The Celebration.*
The Tower of Glass.
ANTÓNIO LOBO ANTUNES, *Knowledge of Hell.*
The Splendor of Portugal.
ALAIN ARIAS-MISSON, *Theatre of Incest.*
JOHN ASHBERY AND JAMES SCHUYLER, *A Nest of Ninnies.*
ROBERT ASHLEY, *Perfect Lives.*
GABRIELA AVIGUR-ROTEM, *Heatwave and Crazy Birds.*
DJUNA BARNES, *Ladies Almanack.*
Ryder.
JOHN BARTH, *LETTERS.*
Sabbatical.
DONALD BARTHELME, *The King.*
Paradise.
SVETISLAV BASARA, *Chinese Letter.*
MIQUEL BAUÇÀ, *The Siege in the Room.*
RENÉ BELLETTO, *Dying.*
MAREK BIEŃCZYK, *Transparency.*
ANDREI BITOV, *Pushkin House.*
ANDREJ BLATNIK, *You Do Understand.*
LOUIS PAUL BOON, *Chapel Road.*
My Little War.
Summer in Termuren.
ROGER BOYLAN, *Killoyle.*
IGNÁCIO DE LOYOLA BRANDÃO, *Anonymous Celebrity.*
Zero.
BONNIE BREMSER, *Troia: Mexican Memoirs.*
CHRISTINE BROOKE-ROSE, *Amalgamemnon.*
BRIGID BROPHY, *In Transit.*
GERALD L. BRUNS, *Modern Poetry and the Idea of Language.*
GABRIELLE BURTON, *Heartbreak Hotel.*
MICHEL BUTOR, *Degrees.*
Mobile.
G. CABRERA INFANTE, *Infante's Inferno.*
Three Trapped Tigers.
JULIETA CAMPOS, *The Fear of Losing Eurydice.*
ANNE CARSON, *Eros the Bittersweet.*
ORLY CASTEL-BLOOM, *Dolly City.*
LOUIS-FERDINAND CÉLINE, *Castle to Castle.*
Conversations with Professor Y.
London Bridge.
Normance.
North.
Rigadoon.
MARIE CHAIX, *The Laurels of Lake Constance.*
HUGO CHARTERIS, *The Tide Is Right.*
ERIC CHEVILLARD, *Demolishing Nisard.*
MARC CHOLODENKO, *Mordechai Schamz.*
JOSHUA COHEN, *Witz.*
EMILY HOLMES COLEMAN, *The Shutter of Snow.*
ROBERT COOVER, *A Night at the Movies.*
STANLEY CRAWFORD, *Log of the S.S. The Mrs Unguentine.*
Some Instructions to My Wife.
RENÉ CREVEL, *Putting My Foot in It.*
RALPH CUSACK, *Cadenza.*
NICHOLAS DELBANCO, *The Count of Concord.*
Sherbrookes.
NIGEL DENNIS, *Cards of Identity.*
PETER DIMOCK, *A Short Rhetoric for Leaving the Family.*
ARIEL DORFMAN, *Konfidenz.*
COLEMAN DOWELL,
Island People.
Too Much Flesh and Jabez.
ARKADII DRAGOMOSHCHENKO, *Dust.*
RIKKI DUCORNET, *The Complete Butcher's Tales.*
The Fountains of Neptune.
The Jade Cabinet.
Phosphor in Dreamland.
WILLIAM EASTLAKE, *The Bamboo Bed.*
Castle Keep.
Lyric of the Circle Heart.
JEAN ECHENOZ, *Chopin's Move.*
STANLEY ELKIN, *A Bad Man.*
Criers and Kibitzers, Kibitzers and Criers.
The Dick Gibson Show.
The Franchiser.
The Living End.
Mrs. Ted Bliss.
FRANÇOIS EMMANUEL, *Invitation to a Voyage.*
SALVADOR ESPRIU, *Ariadne in the Grotesque Labyrinth.*
LESLIE A. FIEDLER, *Love and Death in the American Novel.*
JUAN FILLOY, *Op Oloop.*
ANDY FITCH, *Pop Poetics.*
GUSTAVE FLAUBERT, *Bouvard and Pécuchet.*
KASS FLEISHER, *Talking out of School.*
FORD MADOX FORD, *The March of Literature.*
JON FOSSE, *Aliss at the Fire.*
Melancholy.
MAX FRISCH, *I'm Not Stiller.*
Man in the Holocene.
CARLOS FUENTES, *Christopher Unborn.*
Distant Relations.
Terra Nostra.
Where the Air Is Clear.
TAKEHIKO FUKUNAGA, *Flowers of Grass.*
WILLIAM GADDIS, *J R.*
The Recognitions.

SELECTED DALKEY ARCHIVE TITLES

Joseph McElroy,
Night Soul and Other Stories.
Abdelwahab Meddeb, *Talismano.*
Gerhard Meier, *Isle of the Dead.*
Herman Melville, *The Confidence-Man.*
Amanda Michalopoulou, *I'd Like.*
Steven Millhauser, *The Barnum Museum.*
In the Penny Arcade.
Ralph J. Mills, Jr., *Essays on Poetry.*
Momus, *The Book of Jokes.*
Christine Montalbetti, *The Origin of Man.*
Western.
Olive Moore, *Spleen.*
Nicholas Mosley, *Accident.*
Assassins.
Catastrophe Practice.
Experience and Religion.
A Garden of Trees.
Hopeful Monsters.
Imago Bird.
Impossible Object.
Inventing God.
Judith.
Look at the Dark.
Natalie Natalia.
Serpent.
Time at War.
Warren Motte,
Fables of the Novel: French Fiction since 1990.
Fiction Now: The French Novel in the 21st Century.
Oulipo: A Primer of Potential Literature.
Gerald Murnane, *Barley Patch.*
Inland.
Yves Navarre, *Our Share of Time.*
Sweet Tooth.
Dorothy Nelson, *In Night's City.*
Tar and Feathers.
Eshkol Nevo, *Homesick.*
Wilfrido D. Nolledo, *But for the Lovers.*
Flann O'Brien, *At Swim-Two-Birds.*
The Best of Myles.
The Dalkey Archive.
The Hard Life.
The Poor Mouth.
The Third Policeman.
Claude Ollier, *The Mise-en-Scène.*
Wert and the Life Without End.
Giovanni Orelli, *Walaschek's Dream.*
Patrik Ouředník, *Europeana.*
The Opportune Moment, 1855.
Boris Pahor, *Necropolis.*
Fernando del Paso, *News from the Empire.*
Palinuro of Mexico.
Robert Pinget, *The Inquisitory.*
Mahu or The Material.
Trio.
Manuel Puig, *Betrayed by Rita Hayworth.*
The Buenos Aires Affair.
Heartbreak Tango.
Raymond Queneau, *The Last Days.*
Odile.
Pierrot Mon Ami.
Saint Glinglin.
Ann Quin, *Berg.*
Passages.
Three.
Tripticks.
Ishmael Reed, *The Free-Lance Pallbearers.*
The Last Days of Louisiana Red.
Ishmael Reed: The Plays.
Juice!
Reckless Eyeballing.
The Terrible Threes.
The Terrible Twos.
Yellow Back Radio Broke-Down.
Jasia Reichardt, *15 Journeys Warsaw to London.*
Noëlle Revaz, *With the Animals.*
João Ubaldo Ribeiro, *House of the Fortunate Buddhas.*
Jean Ricardou, *Place Names.*
Rainer Maria Rilke, *The Notebooks of Malte Laurids Brigge.*
Julián Ríos, *The House of Ulysses.*
Larva: A Midsummer Night's Babel.
Poundemonium.
Procession of Shadows.
Augusto Roa Bastos, *I the Supreme.*
Daniël Robberechts, *Arriving in Avignon.*
Jean Rolin, *The Explosion of the Radiator Hose.*
Olivier Rolin, *Hotel Crystal.*
Alix Cleo Roubaud, *Alix's Journal.*
Jacques Roubaud, *The Form of a City Changes Faster, Alas, Than the Human Heart.*
The Great Fire of London.
Hortense in Exile.
Hortense Is Abducted.
The Loop.
Mathematics:
The Plurality of Worlds of Lewis.
The Princess Hoppy.
Some Thing Black.
Raymond Roussel, *Impressions of Africa.*
Vedrana Rudan, *Night.*
Stig Sæterbakken, *Siamese.*
Self Control.
Lydie Salvayre, *The Company of Ghosts.*
The Lecture.
The Power of Flies.
Luis Rafael Sánchez,
Macho Camacho's Beat.
Severo Sarduy, *Cobra & Maitreya.*
Nathalie Sarraute,
Do You Hear Them?
Martereau.
The Planetarium.

FOR A FULL LIST OF PUBLICATIONS, VISIT:
www.dalkeyarchive.com

SELECTED DALKEY ARCHIVE TITLES

Arno Schmidt, *Collected Novellas.*
Collected Stories.
Nobodaddy's Children.
Two Novels.
Asaf Schurr, *Motti.*
Gail Scott, *My Paris.*
Damion Searls, *What We Were Doing and Where We Were Going.*
June Akers Seese,
Is This What Other Women Feel Too?
What Waiting Really Means.
Bernard Share, *Inish.*
Transit.
Viktor Shklovsky, *Bowstring.*
Knight's Move.
A Sentimental Journey: Memoirs 1917–1922.
Energy of Delusion: A Book on Plot.
Literature and Cinematography.
Theory of Prose.
Third Factory.
Zoo, or Letters Not about Love.
Pierre Siniac, *The Collaborators.*
Kjersti A. Skomsvold, *The Faster I Walk, the Smaller I Am.*
Josef Škvorecký, *The Engineer of Human Souls.*
Gilbert Sorrentino,
Aberration of Starlight.
Blue Pastoral.
Crystal Vision.
Imaginative Qualities of Actual Things.
Mulligan Stew.
Pack of Lies.
Red the Fiend.
The Sky Changes.
Something Said.
Splendide-Hôtel.
Steelwork.
Under the Shadow.
W. M. Spackman, *The Complete Fiction.*
Andrzej Stasiuk, *Dukla.*
Fado.
Gertrude Stein, *The Making of Americans.*
A Novel of Thank You.
Lars Svendsen, *A Philosophy of Evil.*
Piotr Szewc, *Annihilation.*
Gonçalo M. Tavares, *Jerusalem.*
Joseph Walser's Machine.
Learning to Pray in the Age of Technique.
Lucian Dan Teodorovici,
Our Circus Presents . . .
Nikanor Teratologen, *Assisted Living.*
Stefan Themerson, *Hobson's Island.*
The Mystery of the Sardine.
Tom Harris.
Taeko Tomioka, *Building Waves.*
John Toomey, *Sleepwalker.*
Jean-Philippe Toussaint, *The Bathroom.*
Camera.
Monsieur.
Reticence.
Running Away.
Self-Portrait Abroad.
Television.
The Truth about Marie.
Dumitru Tsepeneag, *Hotel Europa.*
The Necessary Marriage.
Pigeon Post.
Vain Art of the Fugue.
Esther Tusquets, *Stranded.*
Dubravka Ugresic, *Lend Me Your Character.*
Thank You for Not Reading.
Tor Ulven, *Replacement.*
Mati Unt, *Brecht at Night.*
Diary of a Blood Donor.
Things in the Night.
Álvaro Uribe and Olivia Sears, eds.,
Best of Contemporary Mexican Fiction.
Eloy Urroz, *Friction.*
The Obstacles.
Luisa Valenzuela, *Dark Desires and the Others.*
He Who Searches.
Paul Verhaeghen, *Omega Minor.*
Aglaja Veteranyi, *Why the Child Is Cooking in the Polenta.*
Boris Vian, *Heartsnatcher.*
Llorenç Villalonga, *The Dolls' Room.*
Toomas Vint, *An Unending Landscape.*
Ornela Vorpsi, *The Country Where No One Ever Dies.*
Austryn Wainhouse, *Hedyphagetica.*
Curtis White, *America's Magic Mountain.*
The Idea of Home.
Memories of My Father Watching TV.
Requiem.
Diane Williams, *Excitability: Selected Stories.*
Romancer Erector.
Douglas Woolf, *Wall to Wall.*
Ya! & John-Juan.
Jay Wright, *Polynomials and Pollen.*
The Presentable Art of Reading Absence.
Philip Wylie, *Generation of Vipers.*
Marguerite Young, *Angel in the Forest.*
Miss MacIntosh, My Darling.
Reyoung, *Unbabbling.*
Vlado Žabot, *The Succubus.*
Zoran Živković, *Hidden Camera.*
Louis Zukofsky, *Collected Fiction.*
Vitomil Zupan, *Minuet for Guitar.*
Scott Zwiren, *God Head.*